JAMES GRADY

SIX DAYS

OF THE

CONDOR

WARNER BOOKS

A Time Warner Company

WARNER BOOKS EDITION

Copyright © 1974 by W. W. Norton & Company, Inc.
All rights reserved.

This Warner Books Edition is published by arrangement with the author.

Cover illustration and design by Miles Sprinzan
Cover lettering by Carl Dellacroce

Warner Books, Inc.
666 Fifth Avenue
New York, N.Y. 10103

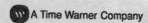 A Time Warner Company

Printed in the United States of America

First Warner Books Printing: October, 1991

10 9 8 7 6 5 4 3 2 1

For a lot of people, including the folks,
Shirley, who helped,
and Rick, who suffered through it

These Days of the Condor

Every novel is cradled by history. This is as true for *Six Days of the Condor* that I wrote on a battered manual typewriter in the depths of the Cold War as it is for any novel being written today on a flickering personal computer while trucks haul away the rubble of the Berlin Wall.

Condor was written to paranoia's metronome—1972; hydrogen bombs were poised to fall. J. Edgar Hoover's FBI knew everything about everybody. Mainland China was inscrutable. The Soviet Union was an evil Gulag wasteland behind an Iron Curtain. *Made In Japan* wasn't funny anymore. Hitler might not be hiding in Paraguay, but the escaped Nazi network *Odessa* had fanatic operatives in Swiss banks and at remote communes. Israeli avengers stalked the globe; they got Eichmann, they could get anybody. Apartheid bedeviled South Africa. South American drug dealers were still small-time businessmen, but the Godfather had a French connection and no one dared refuse his offers. "Terrorists" were more than likely called "revolutionaries," whether they wore KKK robes, Black Panther berets, the *kufiah* of the PLO or clinched long hair and love beads from the dead days of the Sixties—you never knew where they'd strike, who they'd kill, or for certain, *why*. Something called the ozone layer was in jeopardy because of what we sprayed in our armpits in the desperate search for love and social acceptance. A "third-rate burglary" in Washington was turning President Nixon's men into dominos crashing ever closer to their commander in chief, while in Vietnam—TV clips of mountains and jungles, deltas and ancient cities, helicopters—my generation was in the thirteenth year of Americans killing and dying.

Only the mad did not feel any fear.

Love and danger are the strongest intoxicants for a writer's imagination. Like most young men, I knew little about love. Luckily, I knew enough not to indulge my ignorance in my prose.

But danger... In those electric times, a young writer with a fevered imagination needed to know very little to weave a tale out of the air around him.

I wrote *Condor* in four months, working a Montana day job and typing my heart out nights and weekends, approaching that first novel like the journalist I'd been schooled to be. I was twenty-four, and didn't know how ridiculous it was to dream that I could write a book that would be published. In truth, the long odds of reality didn't matter. I had no choice about being a writer, about *writing*. I'd dictated stories to my mother when I was four (she threw them away), and after half a dozen years of unsuccessfully bombarding magazines with poems and short stories, a novel was my next inevitable step.

Good fiction is an ambush for both reader and author.

I walked the battleground that begat *Condor* a year

before I started pounding my keyboard: 1971. I was a college senior, a Sears Congressional Journalism Intern, one of twenty Woodstock warriors brought on fellowship from the hinterland universities of America to the wonders of Washington, D.C., there to work days on a Congressional staff and be taught at night by a new genre of journalists called *investigative reporters*. I lived on A Street, Southeast, six blocks from the white icing Capitol dome that looked even grander than it had on my high school civics textbook. I rented a third-floor garret in a massive row house. A seldom seen man rented the other unit on my floor. At night, through the thin walls, I heard him coughing and wheezing. Fearing tubecular contamination, I learned to shower while standing on my tiptoes in the bathroom we shared.

Every weekday I brushed my recently barbered, acceptably short hair, put on my new suit and one of three garish, hand-wide ties, struggled into a box-shaped tan overcoat, and walked through winter streets to my wondrous intern job on the staff of populist United States Senator Lee Metcalf.

And every day, I walked past a blockish, flat fronted, white stucco townhouse set back from the corner of A and Fourth Streets, Southeast. A short, black-iron fence marked the border of the public sidewalk and that building's domain. Blinds obscured the windows. Then as now, a bronze plaque by the solid door proclaimed the building as the headquarters of the eminently respectable American Historical Association.

But I never saw anyone go in or out of that building.

Then, as I walked to work one grey day, a sniper's bullet cracked my skull: *Wouldn't it be great if that building were a CIA front?*

Wounded, reeling, I fell into the era's paranoia: *What if when I came from lunch, everyone in my office had been murdered?*

It could happen to anyone.

But if it happened to a spy...

My fantasy about a covert CIA office on Capitol Hill was not without foundation in reality. In those days, a flat-faced, grey concrete building with an always-lowered garage door and a windowless, locked entrance sat amidst colorful liquor stores, restaurants and bookstores along the strip of Pennsylvania Avenue that angled out from the Capitol and the House office buildings. No sign identified the concrete edifice to the Congressional aides and tourists strolling past it every day, but several thousand of us shared the secret that the building belonged to the FBI. If you had enough official clout to ask the Bureau, you were told that this Capitol Hill office was one of their translation centers.

Sure, thousands of us thought, *but what do they really do there?* Conventional paranoia claimed the building was the center for the Bureau's bugging of Congressional offices and telephones—a nightmare the FBI vehemently denies.

The question of what the real spooks in the FBI were doing on Capitol Hill was quickly overshadowed in my mind by the question of what the CIA employees stationed in *my* Capitol Hill townhouse were doing.

The reality of most espionage activitiy makes poor fiction. As President Lyndon Johnson noted at the swearing-in ceremony of CIA Director Richard Helms: "...most significant triumphs come not in the secrets passed in the dark, but in patient reading, hour after hour, of highly technical periodicals."

Such ordinary reality is not the meat of drama. Drama occurs when reality breaks down. Or at the edge of the ordinary, where determined people confront cause and effect, deal with their consciences and wrestle fate.

Condor was conceived when James Bond, superspy, dominated that genre. Despite fine movies having been made from their excellent books, masters-in-the-making John Le Carrè (*The Spy Who Came In From The Cold*) and Len Deighton (*The Ipcress File*) were overshadowed by 007. Eric Ambler, Josef Conrad, and Graham Greene could be found on library shelves, but at bookstores, they were blanked out by the glitz of *Dr. No, Goldfinger, From Russia With Love*—Sean Connery and Ursula Andress, sex and a Walther PPK.

As much as I loved "Bond, James Bond," I didn't want to write about a superhero. A superhero always triumphs—is immune to paranoia. Is never in ultimate jeopardy.

And was someone whom I'd never met. Apprentice journalist that I was, I wanted to keep one hand on facts while I shaped my fiction. So I knew that whoever my hero was in that novel that ambushed me on a Washington Street, he was no superman.

But he did work for the CIA.

The Central Intelligence Agency. America's best-known spy shop. In those post-McCarthy days, when our murdered president John Kennedy had publicly loved James Bond and been secretly entangled in best-and-brightest covert intrigues, the CIA was an invisible creature of mythic proportions.

These days, entire bookstores are devoted to tomes on the CIA and spies. Until Vietnam war protests and Watergate helped expose the CIA scandals of the 1970s, the average bookstore carried no books about the Agency. When I researched *Condor*, I found only three credible books on the CIA, two by David Wise and Thomas Ross (*The Invisible*

Government and *The Espionage Establishment*) and one by Andrew Tully (*CIA: The Inside Story*).

Fictionally, the CIA was treated like a ghost, a giant presence everyone tiptoed around but no one touched. Its agents made appearances in hundreds of novels, but they were usually somber creatures of unquestioned monomania and solid competence. *What* and *how* and *why* they did what they did went unexamined. CIA agents were *ipso facto* on the right side; if not Yale superheroes, certainly dependable Boy Scouts tinged with romanticism.

A notable exception was the 1971 novel (that I hadn't read before writing *Condor*) called *The Rope Dancer*, written by Victor Marchetti—a CIA agent who in post-*Condor* 1974 co-authored *The CIA and the Cult of Intelligence*, a classic exposé that a First Amendment-loving Supreme Court censored on a word-by-word basis. In his novel, Marchetti followed a then-frequent and today absurd-sounding practice: he changed the name of the CIA to the NIA, further distancing fiction from reality.

Even Hollywood treated the CIA with a kind of Tinkerbell touch: on screen, the CIA meant impossible mission gadgets, trenchcoated knights in righteous pursuit of a Holy Grail. An engrossing exception that few people, including me, saw at the box office was the 1972 movie *Scorpio*, starring Burt Lancaster as a CIA executive who may or may not deserve the assassin the Agency has forced to hunt him.

One truth about the espionage genre is that many "spy" stories are not about espionage. James Bond was called a spy, but his missions were more those of a global cop. He fought heroin dealers; in real life, spies are more likely to work with or at most try to co-opt fellow black marketeers like drug dealers. In the tradition of Conrad and Somerset Maugham, Don Delillo and Robert Stone may write beautifully about men who use covert means to effect international policy—the great secret "non-spy" activity that the CIA hates to see discussed—but such novels are rare in Cold War literature. Spies, intelligence officers, operatives, analysts and those who do the patient reading praised by LBJ are hard creatures to fictionalize—witness the fact that we have only one, perfect George Smiley.

So even though inspiration had ambushed me with two wonderful components for a novel, I still lacked what Alfred Hitchcock called the MacGuffin, the *why*, the break in ordinary life that would propel my novel's story.

Until the crusades of a muckraker, a Beat poet, and a brave historian lit the darkness of my imagination.

The last lecturer to my 1971 class of Congressional interns was Les Whitten, a novelist and partner to Jack Anderson, whose syndicated column ran in almost a thousand newspapers. Les was the epitome of a muckraker—a term of honor. Neither of us imagined that four years later, after *Condor*, we would be colleagues working together for Anderson's investigative column. That night in 1971, I was only a college kid. After class, I persuaded Les to tell me the "CIA" story he would be breaking in the column after I left Washington for my hometown of Shelby, Montana, where there was no daily newspaper.

Allen Ginsberg is *the* Beat poet. By 1971, as America rolled toward a narcotics nightmare that none of us back then could imagine, he had seen the best minds of his generation destroyed by madness, dragging themselves through America's streets in search of an *angry fix*. The horrors of heroin screamed too loudly for the man inside the poet to ignore. Cherubic, bald, bearded, homosexual, mantra-chanting Ginsberg, hated by thousands of conservative upholders of law, order and *our decent way of life*, did what few of his critics would ever dare to do: Ginsberg declared a personal war on heroin. And he backed his rhetoric with action. His crusade was investigatory as well as proselytory; Les's story concerned Ginsberg's investigations into the CIA's allies in Southeast Asia and their ties to the heroin business.

As Les whispered his news to me, I felt the invisible beast of the CIA shudder.

A year later, as I weighed my ability to sell a novel about a CIA in which not everyone was red-white-and-blue pure, I stumbled across a book by historian Alfred W. McCoy, who braved the wrath of the U.S. government, French intelligence agencies, the Mafia, the Union Corse (the major French criminal syndicate), the Chinese Triads and our exiled Kuomintang Chinese *allies* to write *The Politics of Heroin in Southeast Asia*, an analytical history of the twentieth century whose depth, accuracy and brilliance deserves the Pulitzer and all the other prizes it never received. McCoy tramped the mountains of Laos, air-conditioned government corridors of Saigon and along the *klongs* of Bangkok to gather an irrefutable preponderance of evidence that showed how, in the crusade against communism, our government had *in the least* embraced ignorance about the gangsterism of those who called themselves our friends.

McCoy's book was the final ray of light I needed to see the path of my novel. *Condor* took wing.

Every novel is two books: the one the author writes, and the one that publishers, editors, and the author carve for the reader. In the process of creating that second book, the author is both beef and butcher.

The novel *Six Days of the Condor* that I wrote differs from the novel my publishers printed. *Condor* originally was the tale of a bookish, mildly rebellious researcher who stumbles onto a heroin smuggling ring run by renegade operatives within the CIA. He is assigned to analyze novels for an obscure branch of the CIA—exposed by David Wise and Thomas Ross in their first nonfiction book on espionage—and his office is in a discreet CIA townhouse on Capitol Hill falsely identified as the headquarters for the American Literary Historical Association.

Most of my "revelations" about the CIA came from Wise and Ross; the rest came from my assuming that the CIA, as a government bureaucracy, would function not too differently from other government bureaucracies—like HUD. I projected certain elements, like the existence of a "panic line" for agents in trouble, that later days revealed to be true.

It was those projections, the novel's attitude about the heretofore invisible beast called the CIA, that made it at times almost unique.

My protagonist was deliberately not a superhero; he was *anyman*, any reader, trapped by the paranoia of our times. I chose "Condor" for his codename because it elegantly implies a witness to death; "vulture" sounds gross. Escaping lunchtime assassination by a fluke, Condor finds betrayal waiting within his colleagues when he calls for help. To survive, he must become the kind of field operative he'd only read about in novels and seen in movies. In the end, he perseveres only because of a miscalculated manipulation of the hired assassin who'd originally tried to kill him. In order to reclaim his soul and to revenge the murders of his colleagues and an innocent woman he'd dragooned into helping him, *Condor* becomes an assassin.

And as first written, the novel had a prologue and epilogue set in Vietnam—where so much begins and ends for my generation.

Well. As a journalist and a first-time author, I was

prepared for chain-saw editing of my manuscript (assuming, of course, I could ever get a publisher to read it!). The prose in my manuscript was clipped and simple, and it passed through my editor's hands with less surgery than I'd imagined possible. But the powers that published my first book asked for three major changes: drop the Vietnam prologue and epilogue in favor of immediate story development, let the woman Condor dragoons to help him live ("Killing her is so dark, and his *believing* she's dead is good enough . . ."), and change heroin into something else—"could it be some kind of superdrug? With *The French Connection* just coming out, there's a feeling that heroin has already been done."

I reluctantly agreed to all of those edits: Vietnam was excised, the woman was shot in the head but saved "off-screen" by the miracles of modern medicine, and the bags of heroin smuggled in book crates became morphine bricks— an intrinsically silly revision: nobody smuggles morphine bricks, they refine them into heroin.

Theoretically, I can argue that those three edits *lessened* the book. But such abstract judgements ignore an important truth of writing: prose consists of two equally decisive forces—an idea and its execution. Eighteen years after the fact, I believe that my *ideas* were correct and good, but I can't swear that the writing skills of the twenty-four-year-old I was then could execute those ideas well enough to merit their survival.

Some novels are three books: the author's original work, the edited published volume—and the story Hollywood projects on the silver screen.

No novelist has been better served by Hollywood's hands than I.

And few stories adapted from novels to film have been

more influenced by history's cradle than *Condor*.

The movie based on a book eclipses the book; that's a twentieth-century marketing phenomenon, not an aesthetic judgement. More people go more often to movies than read books. Television and VCRs have multiplied that syndrome.

Hundreds of times, I have been introduced as: "the author of that Robert Redford movie."

Six Days became *Three Days*: cinematic necessity (two hours maximum film running time chopped up into six consecutive days of action would befuddle an audience) and great screenwriting by Lorenzo Semple, Jr., and David Rayfiel. The action moved from Washington, D.C., to New York: that there were CIA agents there, too, added to the paranoia.

And between my completion of the novel and the filming of the movie, history shifted, dramatically and powerfully. The screenwriters couldn't have conjured up such inspiration: a global oil crisis.

What a MacGuffin! Unlike drugs, it had never *been done*.

Throw in Redford—and Faye Dunaway, Cliff Robertson, Max von Sydow, John Houseman, Tina Chen. Put Sidney Pollack behind the camera.

Then come sit in the audience.

With me.

Awe is the only way to describe seeing fantasies you created out of thin air projected onto a movie screen in a theater full of strangers. Who like what they see almost as much as you love it. Awe, and a frightening kind of reverence, the insight of how lucky you are that it all happened in the first place, let alone happened so marvelously *well*.

The power of a *Condor*, of any novel or movie, comes

from more than the talents and skills of author and editor, of screenwriter and director and actors. The power for all fiction comes from something deeper, from an alignment, if you will, with the underlying forces of reality. *Credibility* is an incomplete expression of this alignment.

Credibility is more than facts and beyond truth—it's *what could be*. No matter how strange, wonderful or terrifying, *what could be* is always cradled by *what is*, by history.

Today's history, claim some literary pundits, is in danger of failing to provide substance for today's writers.

Condor was created in 1972. This is 1990. The old realities do not lie in ambush for writers anymore, but the same underlying forces are there: greed, fear, heroism, love, hatred, sacrifice, paranoia.

The Cold War is gone and *no more Vietnams* is a perpetual bi-partisan political promise, but as I write, the 82nd Airborne and the Marines are dug into the sands of the Middle East—because of a love of freedom or because of an oil crisis, or maybe because of both. China is inscrutable. The Soviet Union is being reborn or dying, depending on what time it is. Despite obituaries from respected journalists, the Mafia is alive and well, with its unconvictable Godfather starring on Best Dressed lists as his corporate enterprise faces challenges from the Yakuza, the Triads, the Ghost Shadows, and cocaine cartels in Medelín and Cali. *Made In Japan* is even less of a joke. Hitler is probably dead, but where is Carlos the Jackal? Apartheid bedevils South Africa. Terrorists have no more disappeared than rats. Chile and Argentina are facing their yesterdays of torture. El Salvador, Guatemala and Nicaragua stare straight ahead. Cambodian earth awaits another scarlet rain. Hundreds of thousands of Americans call the streets home, stare with hollow eyes at those of us who can afford to buy a newspaper—what will fill that gaze? Fifty thousand children starved to death last week. Fifty thousand will starve to death this week.

Incredible. True. History's cradle for tomorrow's *Condors*.

RIVER OF DARKNESS, James Grady's first novel of espionage since the movie fifteen years ago based on his first novel, will be published by Warner Books next year.

Preface

The events described in this novel are fictitious, at least to the author's best knowledge. Whether these events might take place is another question, for the structure and operations of the intelligence community are based on fact. Malcolm's branch of the CIA and the 54/12 Group do indeed exist, though perhaps no longer under the designations given to them here.

For the factual background to this story, the author is indebted to the following sources: Jack Anderson, "Washington Merry-Go-Round" (various dates); Alfred W. McCoy, *The Politics of Heroin in Southeast Asia* (1972); Andrew Tully, *CIA: The Inside Story* (1962); David Wise and Thomas B. Ross, *The Invisible Government* (1964) and *The Espionage Establishment* (1967).

". . . most significant triumphs come not in the secrets passed in the dark, but in patient reading, hour after hour, of highly technical periodicals. In a real sense they [the "patriotic and dedicated" CIA researchers] are America's professional students. They are unsung just as they are invaluable."

— *President Lyndon B. Johnson, on swearing in Richard M. Helm as CIA director, June 30, 1966*

Wednesday

Four blocks behind the Library of Congress, just past Southeast A and Fourth Street (one door from the corner), is a white stucco three-story building. Nestled in among the other town houses, it would be unnoticeable if not for its color. The clean brightness stands out among the fading reds, grays, greens, and occasional off-whites. Then, too, the short black iron picket fence and the small, neatly trimmed lawn lend an aura of quiet dignity the other buildings lack. However, few people notice the building. Residents of the area have long since blended it into the familiar neighborhood. The dozens of Capitol Hill and Library of Congress workers who pass it each day don't have time to notice it, and probably wouldn't even if they had time. Located where it is, almost off "the Hill," most of the tourist hordes never come close to it. The few who do are usually looking for a policeman to direct them out of the notoriously rough neighborhood to the safety of national monuments.

If a passerby (for some strange reason) is attracted to the building and takes a closer look, his investigation would reveal very little out of the ordinary. As he stood outside the picket fence, he would probably first note a raised bronze plaque, about three feet by two feet, which proclaims the building to be the national headquarters of the American Literary Historical Society. In Washington, D.C., a city of hundreds of landmarks and headquarters for a multitude of organizations, such a building is not extraordinary. Should the passerby have an eye for architecture and design, he would be pleasantly intrigued by the ornate black wooden door flawed by a curiously large peephole. If our passerby's curiosity is not hampered by shyness, he might open the gate. He probably will not notice the slight click as the magnetic hinge moves from its resting place and breaks an electric circuit. A few short paces later, our passerby mounts the black iron steps to the stoop and rings the bell.

If, as is usually the case, Walter is drinking coffee in the small kitchen, arranging crates of books, or sweeping the floor, then the myth of security is not even flaunted. The visitor hears Mrs. Russell's harsh voice bellow "Come in!" just before she punches the buzzer on her desk releasing the electronic lock.

The first thing a visitor to the Society's headquarters notices is its extreme tidiness. As he stands in the stairwell, his eyes are probably level with the top of Walter's desk, a scant four inches from the edge of the well. There are never any papers on Walter's desk, but then, with a steel rein- forced front, it was never meant for paper. When the visitor turns to his right and climbs out of the stairwell, he sees Mrs. Russell. Unlike Walter's work area, her desk spawns paper. It covers the top, protrudes from drawers, and hides her ancient typewriter. Behind the processed forest sits Mrs. Russell. Her gray hair is thin and usually disheveled. In any case, it is too short to be of much help to her face. A horseshoe-shaped brooch dated 1932 adorns what was once a left breast. She smokes constantly.

Strangers who get this far into the Society's headquarters (other than mailmen and delivery boys) are few in number. Those few, after being screened by Walter's stare (if he is there), deal with Mrs. Russell. If the stranger comes for business, she directs him to the proper person, provided she accepts his clearance. If the stranger is merely one of the brave and curious, she delivers a five-minute, inordinately dull lecture on the Society's background of foundation funding, its purpose of literary analysis, advancement, and achievement (referred to as "the 3 A's"), shoves pamphlets into usually less-than-eager hands, states that there is no one present who can answer further questions, suggests writing to an unspecified address for further information, and then bids a brisk "Good day." Visitors are universally stunned by this onslaught and leave meekly, probably without noticing the box on Walter's desk which took their picture or the red light and buzzer above the door which announces the opening of the gate. The visitor's disappointment would dissolve into fantasy should he learn that he had just visited a section branch office of a department in the Central Intelligence Agency's Intelligence Division.

The National Security Act of 1947 created the Central Intelligence Agency, a result of the World War II experience of being caught flat-footed at Pearl Harbor. The Agency, or the Company, as many of its employees call it, is the largest and most active entity in the far-flung American intelligence network, a network composed of eleven major agencies, around two hundred thousand persons, and annually budgeted in the billions of dollars. The CIA's activities, like those of its major counterparts—Britain's MI6, Russia's KGB, and Red China's Social Affairs Department—range through a spectrum of covert espionage, technical research, the funding of loosely linked political action groups, support to friendly governments, and direct paramilitary operations. The wide variety of activities of these agencies, coupled with their basic mission of national security in a troubled world, has made the intelligence agency one of the most important branches of government. In America, former CIA Director Allen Dulles once said, "The National Security Act of 1947 . . . has given Intelligence a more influential position in our government than Intelligence enjoys in any other government of the world."

The main activity of the CIA is simple, painstaking research. Hundreds of researchers daily scour technical journals, domestic and foreign periodicals of all kinds, speeches, and media broadcasts. This research is divided between two of the four divisions of the CIA. The Research Division (RD) is in charge of technical intelligence, and its experts provide detailed reports of the latest scientific advances in all countries, including the United States and its allies. The Intelligence Division (ID) engages in a highly specialized form of scholastic research. About 80 percent of the information ID handles comes from "open" sources: public magazines, broadcasts, journals, and books. ID digests its data and from this fare produces three major types of reports: one type makes long-range projections dealing with areas of interest, a second is a daily review of the current world situation, and the third tries to detect gaps in CIA activities. The research gathered by both ID and RD is used by the other two divisions: Support (the administrative arm which deals with logistics, equipment, security, and communications) and Plans (all covert activities, the actual spying division).

The American Literary Historical Society, with headquarters in Washington and a small receiving office in Seattle, is a section branch of one of the smaller departments in the CIA. Because of the inexact nature of the data the department deals with, it is only loosely allied to ID, and, indeed, to CIA as a whole. The department (officially designated as Department 17, CIAID) reports are not consistently incorporated in any one of the three major research report areas. Indeed, Dr. Lappe, the very serious, very nervous head of the Society (officially titled Section 9, Department 17, CIAID), slaves over weekly, monthly, and annual reports which may not even make the corresponding report of mother Department 17. In turn, Department 17 reports often will not impress major group coordinators on the division level and thus will fail to be incorporated into any of the ID reports. *C'est la vie*.

The function of the Society and of Department 17 is to keep track of all espionage and related acts recorded in literature. In other words, the Department reads spy thrillers and murder mysteries. The antics and situations in thousands of volumes of mystery and mayhem are carefully detailed and analyzed in Department 17 files. Volumes dating as far back as James Fenimore Cooper have been scrutinized. Most of the company-owned volumes are kept at the Langley, Virginia, CIA central complex, but the Society headquarters maintains a library of almost three thousand volumes. At one time the Department was housed in the Christian Heurich Brewery near the State Department, but in the fall of 1961, when CIA moved to its Langley complex, the Department transferred to the Virginia suburbs. In 1970 the ever-increasing volume of pertinent literature began to create logistic and expense problems for the Department. Additionally, the Deputy Director of ID questioned the need for highly screened and, therefore, highly paid analysts. Consequently, the Department reopened its branch section in metropolitan Washington, this time conveniently close to the Library of Congress. Because the employees were not in the central complex, they needed only to pass a cursory Secret clearance rather than the exacting Top Secret clearance required for employment at the complex. Naturally, their salaries paralleled their rating.

The analysts for the Department keep abreast of the literary field and divide their work basically by mutual consent. Each analyst has areas of expertise, areas usually defined by author. In addition to summarizing plots and methods of all the books, the analysts daily receive a series of specially "sanitized" reports from the Langley complex. The reports contain capsule descriptions of actual events with all names deleted and as few necessary details as possible. Fact and fiction are compared, and if major correlations occur, the analyst begins a further investigation with a more detailed but still sanitized report. If the correlation still appears strong, the information and reports are passed on for review to a higher classified section of the Department. Somewhere after that the decision is made as to whether the author was guessing and lucky or whether he knew more than he should. If the latter is the case, the author is definitely unlucky, for then a report is filed with the Plans Division for action. The analysts are also expected to compile lists of helpful tips for agents. These lists are forwarded to Plans Division instructors, who are always looking for new tricks.

Ronald Malcolm was supposed to be working on one of those lists that morning, but instead he sat reversed on a wooden chair, his chin resting on the scratched walnut back. It was fourteen minutes until nine o'clock, and he had been sitting there since he climbed the spiral staircase to his second-story office at 8:30, spilling hot coffee and swearing loudly all the way. The coffee was long gone and Malcolm badly wanted a second cup, but he didn't dare take his eyes off his window.

Barring illness, every morning between 8:40 and 9:00 an incredibly beautiful girl walked up Southeast A, past Malcolm's window, and into the Library of Congress. And every morning, barring illness or unavoidable work, Malcolm watched her for the brief interval it took her to pass out of view. It became a ritual, one that helped Malcolm rationalize getting out of a perfectly comfortable bed to shave and walk to work. At first lust dominated Malcolm's attitude, but this had gradually been replaced by a sense of awe that was beyond his definition. In February he gave up even trying to think about it, and now, two months later, he merely waited and watched.

It was the first real day of spring. Early in the year there had been intervals of sunshine scattered through generally rainy days, but no real spring. Today dawned bright and stayed bright. An aroma promising cherry blossoms crept through the morning smog. Out of the corner of his eye Malcolm saw her coming, and he tipped his chair closer to the window.

The girl didn't walk up the street, she strode, moving with purpose and the pride born of modest yet firm, knowledgeable confidence. Her shiny brown hair lay across her back, sweeping past her broad shoulders to fall halfway to her slender waist. She wore no makeup, and when she wasn't wearing sunglasses one could see how her eyes, large and well-spaced, perfectly matched her straight nose, her wide mouth, her full face, her square chin. The tight brown sweater hugged her large breasts and even without a bra there was no sag. The plaid skirt revealed full thighs, almost too muscular. Her calves flowed to her ankles. Three more firm steps and she vanished from sight.

Malcolm sighed and settled back in his chair. His typewriter had a half-used sheet of paper in the carriage. He rationalized that this represented an adequate start on his morning's work. He belched loudly, picked up his empty cup, and left his little red and blue room.

When he got to the stairs, Malcolm paused. There were two coffeepots in the building, one on the main floor in the little kitchen area behind Mrs. Russell's desk and one on the third floor of the wrapping table at the back of the open stacks. Each pot had its advantages and disadvantages. The first-floor pot was larger and served the most people. Besides Mrs. Russell and ex-drill instructor Walter ("Sergeant Jennings, if you please!"), Dr. Lappe and the new accountant-librarian Heidegger had their offices downstairs, and thus in the great logistical scheme of things used that pot. The coffee was, of course, made by Mrs. Russell, whose many faults did not include poor cooking. There were two disadvantages to the first-floor pot. If Malcolm or Ray Thomas, the other analysts on the second floor, used that pot, they ran the risk of meeting Dr. Lappe. Those meetings were uncomfortable. The other disadvantage was Mrs. Russell and her smell, or, as Ray was wont to call her, Perfume Polly.

Use of the third-floor pot was minimal, as only Harold Martin and Tamatha Reynolds, the other two analysts, were permanently assigned that pot. Sometimes Ray or Malcolm exercised their option. As often as he dared, Walter wandered by for refreshment and a glance at Tamatha's frail form. Tamatha was a nice girl, but she hadn't a clue about making coffee. In addition to subjecting himself to a culinary atrocity by using the third-floor pot, Malcolm risked being cornered by Harold Martin and bombarded with the latest statistics, scores, and opinions from the world of sports, followed by nostalgic stories of high-school prowess. He decided to go downstairs.

Mrs. Russell greeted Malcolm with the usual disdainful grunt as he walked by her desk. Sometimes, just to see if she had changed, Malcolm stopped to "chat" with her. She would shuffle papers, and no matter what Malcolm talked about she rambled through a disjointed monologue dealing with how hard she worked, how sick she was, and how little she was appreciated. This morning Malcolm went no further than a sardonic grin and an exaggerated nod.

Malcolm heard the click of an office door opening just as he started back upstairs with his cup of coffee, and braced himself for a lecture from Dr. Lappe.

"Oh, ah, Mr. Malcolm, may I . . . may I talk to you for a moment?"

Relief. The speaker was Heidegger and not Dr. Lappe. With a smile and a sigh, Malcolm turned to face a slight man so florid that even his bald spot glowed. The inevitable tab-collar white shirt and narrow black tie squeezed the large head from the body.

"Hi, Rich," said Malcolm, "how are you?"

"I'm fine . . . Ron. Fine." Heidegger tittered. Despite six months of total abstinence and hard work, his nerves were still shot. Any inquiry into Heidegger's condition, however polite, brought back the days when he fearfully sneaked drinks in CIA bathrooms, frantically chewing gum to hide the security risk on his breath. After he "volunteered" for cold turkey, traveled through the hell of withdrawal, and began to pick up pieces of his sanity, the doctors told him he had been turned in by the security section in charge of monitoring the rest rooms. "Would you, I mean, could you come in for a second?"

Any distraction was welcome. "Sure, Rich."

They entered the small office reserved for the accountant-librarian and sat, Heidegger behind his desk, Malcolm on the old stuffed chair left by the building's former tenant. For several seconds they sat silent.

Poor little man, thought Malcolm. Scared shitless, still hoping you can work your way back into favor. Still hoping for return of your Top Secret rating so you can move from this dusty green bureaucratic office to another dusty but more Secret office. Maybe, Malcolm thought, if you are lucky, your next office will be one of the other three colors intended to "maximize an efficient office environment," maybe you'll get a nice blue room the same soothing shade as three of my walls and hundreds of other government offices.

"Right!" Heidegger's shout echoed through the room. Suddenly conscious of his volume, he leaned back in his chair and began again. "I . . . I hate to bother you like this . . ."

"Oh, no trouble at all."

"Right. Well, Ron—you don't mind if I call you Ron, do you? Well, as you know, I'm new to this section. I decided to go over the records for the last few years to acquaint myself with the operation." He chuckled nervously. "Dr. Lappe's briefing was, shall we say, less than complete."

Malcolm joined in his chuckle. Anybody who laughed at Dr. Lappe had something on the ball. Malcolm decided he might like Heidegger after all.

He continued, "Right. Well, you've been here two years, haven't you? Ever since the move from Langley?"

Right, thought Malcolm as he nodded. Two years, two months, and some odd days.

"Right. Well, I've found some . . . discrepancies I think need clearing up, and I thought maybe you could help me." Heidegger paused and received a willing but questioning shrug from Malcolm. "Well, I found two funny things—or rather, funny things in two areas.

"The first one has to do with accounts, you know, money paid in and out for expenses, salaries, what have you. You probably don't know anything about that, it's something I'll have to figure out. But the other thing has to do with the books, and I'm checking with you and the other research analysts to see if I can find out anything before I go to Dr. Lappe with my written report." He paused for another encouraging nod. Malcolm didn't disappoint him.

"Have you ever, well, have you ever noticed any missing books? No, wait," he said, seeing the confused look on Malcolm's face, "let me say that again. Do you ever know of an instance where we haven't got books we ordered or books we should have?"

"No, not that I know of," said Malcolm, beginning to

get bored. "If you could tell me which ones are missing, or might be missing..." He let his sentence trail off, and Heidegger took the cue.

"Well, that's just it, I don't really know. I mean, I'm not really sure if any are, and if they are, what they are or even why they are missing. It's all very confusing." Silently, Malcolm agreed.

"You see," Heidegger continued, "sometime in 1968 we received a shipment of books from our Seattle purchasing branch. We received all the volumes they sent, but just by chance I happened to notice that the receiving clerk signed for *five* crates of books. But the billing order—which, I might add, bears both the check marks and signatures of our agent in Seattle *and* the trucking firm—says there were *seven* crates. That means we're missing two crates of books without really missing any books. Do you understand what I mean?"

Lying slightly, Malcolm said, "Yeah, I understand what you're saying, though I think it's probably just a mistake. Somebody, probably the clerk, couldn't count. Anyway, you say we're not missing any books. Why not just let it go?"

"You don't understand!" exclaimed Heidegger, leaning forward and shocking Malcolm with the intensity in his voice. "I'm responsible for these records! When I take over I have to certify I receive everything true and proper. I did that, and this mistake is botching up the records! It looks bad, and if it's ever found I'll get the blame. Me!" By the time he finished, he was leaning across the desk and his volume was again causing echoes.

Malcolm was thoroughly bored. The prospect of listening to Heidegger ramble on about inventory discrepancies did not interest him in the least. Malcolm also didn't like the way Heidegger's eyes burned behind those thick glasses when he got excited. It was time to leave. He leaned toward Heidegger.

"Look, Rich," he said, "I know this mess causes problems for you, but I'm afraid I can't help you out. Maybe one of the other analysts knows something I don't, but I doubt it. If you want my advice, you'll forget the whole thing and cover it up. In case you haven't guessed, that's what your predecessor Johnson always did. If you want to press things, I suggest you don't go to Dr. Lappe. He'll get upset, muddy the whole mess beyond belief, blow it out of proportion, and everybody will be unhappy."

Malcolm stood up and walked to the door. Looking back, he saw a small, trembling man sitting behind an open ledger and a draftsman's light.

Malcolm walked as far as Mrs. Russell's desk before he let out his sigh of relief. He threw what was left of the cold coffee down the sink, and went upstairs to his room, sat down, put his feet up on his desk, farted, and closed his eyes.

When he opened them a minute later he was staring at his Picasso print of Don Quixote. The print appropriately hung on his half-painted red wall. Don Quixote was responsible for Ronald Leonard Malcolm's exciting position as a Central Intelligence agent. Two years.

In September of 1970, Malcolm took his long delayed Master's written examination. Everything went beautifully for the first two hours: he wrote a stirring explanation of Plato's allegory of the cave, analyzed the condition of two of the travelers in Chaucer's *Canterbury Tales*, discussed the significance of rats in Camus's *The Plague*, and faked his way through Holden Caulfield's struggle against homosexuality in *Catcher in the Rye*. Then he turned to the last page and ran into a brick wall that demanded, "Discuss in depth at least three significant incidents in Cervantes' *Don Quixote*, including in the discussion the symbolic meaning of each incident, its relation to the other two incidents and the plot as a whole, and show how Cervantes used these incidents to characterize Don Quixote and Sancho Panza."

Malcolm had never read *Don Quixote*. For five precious minutes he stared at the test. Then, very carefully, he opened a fresh examination book and began to write:

"I have never read *Don Quixote*, but I think he was defeated by a windmill. I am not sure what happened to Sancho Panza.

"The adventures of Don Quixote and Sancho Panza, a team generally regarded as seeking justice, can be compared to the adventures of Rex Stout's two most famous characters, Nero Wolfe and Archie Goodwin. For example, in the classic Wolf adventure *The Black Mountain* . . ."

After finishing a lengthy discussion of Nero Wolfe, using *The Black Mountain* as a focal point, Malcolm turned in his completed examination, went home to his apartment, and contemplated his bare feet.

Two days later he was called to the office of the professor of Spanish Literature. To his surprise, Malcolm was not chastised for his examination answer. Instead, the professor asked Malcolm if he was interested in "murder mysteries." Startled, Malcolm told the truth: reading such books helped him maintain some semblance of sanity in college. Smiling, the professor asked if he would like to "so maintain your sanity for money?" Naturally, Malcolm said, he would. The professor made a phone call, and that day Malcolm lunched with his first CIA agent.

It is not unusual for college professors, deans, and other academic personnel to act as CIA recruiters. In the early 1950s a Yale Coach recruited a student who was later caught infiltrating Red China.

Two months later Malcolm was finally "cleared for limited employment," as are 17 percent of all CIA applicants. After a special, cursory training period, Malcolm walked up the short flight of iron stairs of the American Literary Historical Society to Mrs. Russell, Dr. Lappe, and his first day as a full-fledged intelligence agent.

Malcolm sighed at the wall, his calculated victory over Dr. Lappe. His third day at work, Malcolm quit wearing a suit and tie. One week of gentle hints passed before Dr. Lappe called him in for a little chat about etiquette. While the good Doctor agreed that bureaucracies tended to be a little stifling, he implied that one really should find a method other than "unconventional" dress for letting in the sun. Malcolm said nothing, but the next day he showed up for work early, properly dressed in suit and tie and carrying a large box. By the time Walter reported to Dr. Lappe at ten, Malcolm had almost finished painting one of his walls fire-engine red. Dr. Lappe sat in stunned silence while Malcolm innocently explained his newest method for letting in the sun. When two other analysts began to pop into the office to exclaim their approval, the good Doctor quietly stated that perhaps Malcolm had been right to brighten the individual rather than the institution. Malcolm sincerely and quickly agreed. The red paint and painting equipment moved to the third-floor storage room. Malcolm's suit and tie once more vanished. Dr. Lappe chose individual rebellion rather than inspired collective revolution against government property.

Malcolm sighed to nostalgia before he resumed describing a classic John Dickson Carr method for creating "locked-door" situations.

Meanwhile Heidegger had been busy. He took Malcolm's advice concerning Dr. Lappe, but he was too frightened to try and hide a mistake from the Company. If they could catch you in the bathroom, no place was safe. He also knew that if he could pull a coup, rectify a malfunctioning situation, or at least show he could responsibly recognize problems, his chances of being reinstated in grace would greatly increase. So through ambition and paranoia (always a bad combination) Richard Heidegger made his fatal mistake.

He wrote a short memo to the chief of mother Department 17. In carefully chosen, obscure, but leading terms, he described what he had told Malcolm. All memos were usually cleared through Dr. Lappe, but exceptions were not unknown. Had Heidegger followed the normal course of procedure, everything would have been fine, for Dr. Lappe knew better than to let a memo critical of his section move up the chain of command. Heidegger guessed this, so he personally put the envelope in the delivery bag.

Twice a day, once in the morning and once in the evening, two cars of heavily armed men pick up and deliver intra-agency communications from all CIA substations in the Washington area. The communications are driven the eight miles to Langley, where they are sorted for distribution. Rich's memo went out in the afternoon pickup.

A strange and unorthodox thing happened to Rich's memo. Like all communications to and from the Society, the memo disappeared from the delivery room before the sorting officially began. The memo appeared on the desk of a wheezing man in a spacious east-wing office. The man read it twice, once quickly, then again, very, very slowly. He left the room and arranged for all files pertaining to the Society to disappear and reappear at a Washington location. He then came back and telephoned to arrange a date at a current art exhibit. Next he reported in sick and caught a bus for the city. Within an hour he was engaged in earnest conversation with a distinguished-looking gentleman who might have been a banker. They talked as they strolled up Pennsylvania Avenue.

That night the distinguished-looking gentleman met yet another man, this time in Clyde's, a noisy, crowded Georgetown bar frequented by the Capitol Hill crowd. They too took a walk, stopping occasionally to gaze at reflections in the numerous shopwindows. The second man was also distinguished-looking. Striking is a more correct adjective. Something about his eyes told you he definitely was not a banker. He listened while the first man talked.

"I am afraid we have a slight problem."

"Really?"

"Yes. Weatherby intercepted this today." He handed the second man Heidegger's memo.

The second man had to read it only once. "I see what you mean."

"I knew you would. We really must take care of this, now."

"I will see to it."

"Of course."

"You realize that there may be other complications besides this," the second man said as he gestured with Heidegger's memo, "which may have to be taken care of."

"Yes. Well, that is regrettable, but unavoidable." The second man nodded and waited for the first man to continue. "We must be very sure, completely sure about those complications." Again the second man nodded, waiting. "And there is one other element. Speed. Time is of the absolute essence. Do what you must to follow that assumption."

The second man thought for a moment and then said, "Maximum speed may necessitate . . . cumbersome and sloppy activity."

The first man handed him a portfolio containing all the "disappeared" files and said, "Do what you must."

The two men parted after a brief nod of farewell. The first man walked four blocks and turned the corner before he caught a taxi. He was glad the meeting was over. The second man watched him go, waited a few minutes scanning the passing crowds, then headed for a bar and a telephone.

That morning at 3:15 Heidegger unlocked his door to the knock of police officers. When he opened the door he found two men in ordinary clothes smiling at him. One was very tall and painfully thin. The other was quite distinguished, but if you looked in his eyes you could tell he wasn't a banker.

The two men shut the door behind them.

"These activities have their own rules and methods of concealment which seek to mislead and obscure."

—President Dwight D. Eisenhower, 1960

Thursday, Morning to Early Afternoon

The rain came back Thursday. Malcolm woke with the start of a cold—congested, tender throat and a slightly woozy feeling. In addition to waking up sick, he woke up late. He thought for several minutes before deciding to go to work. Why waste sick time on a cold? He cut himself shaving, couldn't make the hair over his ears stay down, had trouble putting in his right contact lens, and found that his raincoat had disappeared. As he ran the eight blocks to work it dawned on him that he might be too late to see The Girl. When he hit Southeast A, he looked up the block just in time to see her disappear into the Library of Congress. He watched her so intently he didn't look where he was going and he stepped in a deep puddle. He was more embarrassed than angry, but the man he saw in the blue sedan parked just up from the Society didn't seem to notice the blunder. Mrs. Russell greeted Malcolm with a curt " 'Bout time." On the way to his room, he spilled his coffee and burned his hand. Some days you just can't win.

Shortly after ten there was a soft knock on his door,

21

and Tamatha entered his room. She stared at him for a few seconds through her thick glasses, a timid smile on her lips. Her hair was so thin Malcolm thought he could see each individual strand.

"Ron," she whispered, "do you know if Rich is sick?"

"No!" Malcolm yelled, and then loudly blew his nose.

"Well, you don't need to bellow! I'm worried about him. He's not here and he hasn't called in."

"That's too fuckin' bad." Malcolm drew the words out, knowing that swearing made Tamatha nervous.

"What's eating *you*, for heaven's sake?" she said.

"I've got a cold."

"I'll get you an aspirin."

"Don't bother," he said ungraciously. "It wouldn't help."

"Oh, you're impossible! Goodbye!" She left, closing the door smartly behind her.

Sweet Jesus, Malcolm thought, then went back to Agatha Christie.

At 11:15 the phone rang. Malcolm picked it up and heard the cool voice of Dr. Lappe.

"Malcolm, I have an errand for you, and it's your turn to go for lunch. I assume everyone will wish to stay in the building." Malcolm looked out the window at the pouring rain and came to the same conclusion. Dr. Lappe continued. "Consequently, you might as well kill two birds with one stone and pick up lunch on the way back from the errand. Walter is already taking food orders. Since you have to drop a package at the Old Senate Office Building, I suggest you pick up the food at Hap's. You may leave now."

Five minutes later a sneezing Malcolm trudged through

the basement to the coalbin exit at the rear of the building. No one had known the coalbin exit existed, as it hadn't been shown on the original building plans. It stayed hidden until Walter moved a chest of drawers while chasing a rat and found the small, dusty door that opened behind the lilac bushes. The door can't be seen from the outside, but there is enough room to squeeze between the bushes and the wall. The door only opens from the inside.

Malcolm muttered to himself all the way to the Old Senate Office Building. He sniffled between mutters. The rain continued. By the time he reached the building, the rain had changed his suède jacket from a light tan to a black brown. The blond receptionist in the Senator's office took pity on him and gave him a cup of coffee while he dried out. She said he was "officially" waiting for the Senator to confirm delivery of the package. She coincidentally finished counting the books just as Malcolm finished his coffee. The girl smiled nicely, and Malcolm decided delivering murder mysteries to a senator might not be a complete waste.

Normally, it's a five-minute walk from the Old Senate Office Building to Hap's on Pennsylvania Avenue, but the rain had become a torrent, so Malcolm made the trip in three minutes. Hap's is a favorite of Capitol Hill employees because it's quick, tasty, and has its own brand of class. The restaurant is a cross between a small Jewish delicatessen and a Montana bar. Malcolm gave his carry-out list to a waitress, ordered a meatball sandwich and milk for himself.

While Malcolm had been sipping coffee in the Senator's office, a gentleman in a raincoat with his hat hiding much of his face turned the corner from First Street and walked up Southeast A to the blue sedan. The custom-cut raincoat matched the man's striking appearance, but there was no one on the street to notice. He casually but completely scanned the street and buildings, then gracefully climbed in the front seat of the sedan. As he firmly shut the door, he looked at the driver and said, "Well?"

Without taking his eyes off the building, the driver wheezed, "All present or accounted for, sir."

"Excellent. I watch while you phone. Tell them to wait ten minutes, then hit it."

"Yes, sir." The driver began to climb out of the car, but a sharp voice stopped him.

"Weatherby," the man said, pausing for effect, "there will be no mistakes."

Weatherby swallowed. "Yes, sir."

Weatherby walked to the open phone next to the grocery store on the corner of Southeast A and Sixth. In Mr. Henry's, a bar five blocks away on Pennsylvania Avenue, a tall, frightfully thin man answered the bartender's page for "Mr. Wazburn." The man called Wazburn listened to the curt instructions, nodding his assent into the phone. He hung up and returned to his table, where two friends waited. They paid the bill (three brandy coffees), and walked up First Street to an alley just behind Southeast A. At the street light they passed a young, long-haired man in a rain-soaked suède jacket hurrying in the opposite direction. An empty yellow van stood between the two buildings on the edge of the alley. The men climbed in the back and prepared for their morning's work.

Malcolm had just ordered his meatball sandwich when a mailman with his pouch slung in front of him turned the corner at First Street to walk down Southeast A. A stocky man in a bulging raincoat walked stiffly a few paces behind the mailman. Five blocks farther up the street a tall, thin man walked toward the other two. He also wore a bulging raincoat, though on him the coat only reached his knees.

As soon as Weatherby saw the mailman turn onto Southeast A, he pulled out of his parking place and drove away. Neither the men in the car nor the men on the street acknowledged the others' presence. Weatherby sighed relief in between wheezes. He was overjoyed to be through with his part of the assignment. Tough as he was, when he looked at the silent man next to him he was thankful he had made no mistakes.

But Weatherby was wrong. He had made one small, commonplace mistake, a mistake he could have easily avoided. A mistake he should have avoided.

If anyone had been watching, he would have seen three men, two businessmen and a mailman, coincidentally arrive at the Society's gate at the same time. The two businessmen politely let the mailman lead the way to the door and push the button. As usual, Walter was away from his desk (though it probably wouldn't have made any difference if he had been there). Just as Malcolm finished his sandwich at Hap's, Mrs. Russell heard the buzzer and rasped, "Come in."

And with the mailman leading the way, they did.

Malcolm dawdled over his lunch, polishing off his meatball sandwich with the specialty of the house, chocolate rum cake. After his second cup of coffee, his conscience forced him back into the rain. The torrent had subsided into a drizzle. Lunch had improved Malcolm's spirits and his health. He took his time, both because he enjoyed the walk and because he didn't want to drop the three bags of sandwiches. In order to break the routine, he walked down Southeast A on the side opposite the Society. His decision gave him a better view of the building as he approached, and consequently he knew something was wrong much earlier than he normally would have.

It was a little thing that made Malcolm wonder. A small detail quite out of place yet so insignificant it appeared meaningless. But Malcolm noticed little things, like the open window on the third floor. The Society's windows are rolled out rather than pushed up, so the open window jutted out from the building. When Malcolm first saw the window the significance didn't register, but when he was a block and a half away it struck him and he stopped.

It is not unusual for windows in the capital to be open, even on a rainy day. Washington is usually warm, even during spring rains. But since the Society building is air-conditioned, the only reason to open a window is for fresh air. Malcolm knew the fresh-air explanation was absurd—absurd because of the particular window that stood open. Tamatha's window.

Tamatha—as everyone in the section knew—lived in terror of open windows. When she was nine, her two teen-age brothers had fought over a picture the three of them had found while exploring the attic. The older brother had slipped on a rug and had plunged out the attic window to the street below, breaking his neck and becoming paralyzed for life. Tamatha had once confided in Malcolm that only a fire, rape, or murder would make her go near any open window. Yet her office window stood wide open.

Malcolm tried to quell his uneasiness. Your damn overactive imagination, he thought. It's probably open for a perfectly good reason. Maybe somebody is playing a joke on her. But no staff member played practical jokes, and he knew no one would tease Tamatha in that manner. He walked slowly down the street, past the building, and to the corner. Everything else seemed in order. He heard no noise in the building, but then they were all probably reading.

This is silly, he thought. He crossed the street and quickly walked to the gate, up the steps, and, after a moment's hesitation, rang the bell. Nothing. He heard the bell ring inside the building, but Mrs. Russell didn't answer. He rang again. Still nothing. Malcolm's spine began to tingle and his neck felt cold.

Walter is shifting books, he thought, and Perfume Polly is taking a shit. They must be. Slowly he reached in his pocket for the key. When anything is inserted in the keyhole during the day, buzzers ring and lights flash all over the building. At night they also ring in Washington police headquarters, the Langley complex, and a special security house in downtown Washington. Malcolm heard the soft buzz of the bells as he turned the lock. He swung the door open and quickly stepped inside.

From the bottom of the stairwell Malcolm could only see that the room appeared to be empty. Mrs. Russell wasn't at her desk. Out of the corner of his eye he noticed that Dr. Lappe's door was partially open. There was a peculiar odor in the room. Malcolm tossed the sandwich bags on top of Walter's desk and slowly mounted the stairs.

He found the sources of the odor. As usual, Mrs. Russell had been standing behind her desk when they entered. The blast from the machine gun in the mailman's pouch had knocked her almost as far back as the coffeepot. Her cigarette had dropped on her neck, singeing her flesh until the last millimeter of tobacco and paper had oxidized. A strange dullness came over Malcolm as he stared at the huddled flesh in the pool of blood. An automaton, he slowly turned and walked into Dr. Lappe's office.

Walter and Dr. Lappe had been going over invoices when they heard strange coughing noises and the thump of Mrs. Russell's body hitting the floor. Walter opened the door to help her pick up the dropped delivery (he heard the buzzer and Mrs. Russell say, "What have you got for us today?"). The last thing he saw was a tall, thin man holding an L-shaped device. The postmortem revealed that Walter took a short burst, five rounds in the stomach. Dr. Lappe saw the whole thing, but there was nowhere to run. His body slumped against the far wall beneath a row of bloody diagonal holes.

Two of the men moved quietly upstairs, leaving the mailman to guard the door. None of the other staff had heard a thing. Otto Skorzeny, Hitler's chief commando, once demonstrated the effectiveness of a silenced British sten gun by firing a clip behind a batch of touring generals. The German officers never heard a thing, but they refused to copy the British weapon, as the Third Reich naturally made better devices. These men were satisfied with the sten. The tall man flung open Malcolm's door and found an empty office. Ray Thomas was behind his desk on his knees picking up a dropped pencil when the stocky man found him. Ray had time to scream, "Oh, my God, no...," before his brain exploded.

Tamatha and Harold Martin heard Ray scream, but they had no idea why. Almost simultaneously they opened their doors and ran to the head of the stairs. All was quiet for a moment; then they heard the soft shuffle of feet slowly climbing the stairs. The steps stopped, then a very faint metallic *click, snap, twang* jarred them from their lethargy. They couldn't have known the exact source of the sound (a new ammunition clip being inserted and the weapon being armed), but they instinctively knew what it meant. They both ran into their rooms, slamming the doors behind them.

Harold showed the most presence of mind. He locked his door and dialed three digits before the stocky man kicked the door open and cut him down.

Tamatha reacted on a different instinct. For years she thought only a major emergency could get her to open a window. Now she knew such an emergency was on her. She frantically rolled the window open, looking for escape, looking for help, looking for anything. Dizzied by the height, she took her glasses off and laid them on her desk. She heard Harold's door splinter, a rattling cough, the thump, and fled again to the window. Her door slowly opened.

For a long time nothing happened, then slowly Tamatha turned to face the thin man. He hadn't fired for fear a slug would fly out the window, hit something, and draw attention to the building. He would risk that only if she screamed. She didn't. She saw only a blur, but she knew the blur was motioning her away from the window. She moved slowly toward her desk. If I'm going to die, she thought, I want to see. Her hand reached out for her glasses, and she raised them to her eyes. The tall man waited until they were in place and comprehension registered on her face. Then he squeezed the trigger, holding it tight until the last shell from the full clip exploded, ejecting the spent casing out of the side of the gun. The bullets kept Tamatha dancing, bouncing between the wall and the filing cabinet, knocking her glasses off, disheveling her hair. The thin man watched her riddled body slowly slide to the floor, then he turned to join his stocky companion, who had just finished checking the rest of the floor. They took their time going downstairs.

While the mailman maintained his vigil on the door, the stocky man searched the basement. He found the coalbin door but thought nothing of it. He should have, but then his error was partially due to Weatherby's mistake. The stocky man did find and destroy the telephone switchbox. An inoperative phone causes less alarm than a phone unanswered. The tall man searched Heidegger's desk. The material he sought should have been in the third drawer, left-hand side, and it was. He also took a manila envelope. He dumped a handful of shell casings in the envelope with a small piece of paper he took from his jacket pocket. He sealed the envelope and wrote on the outside. His gloves made writing difficult, but he wanted to disguise his handwriting anyway. The scrawl designated the envelope as a personal package for "Lockenvar, Langley headquarters." The stocky man opened the camera and exposed the film. The tall man contemptuously tossed the envelope on Mrs. Russell's desk. He and his companions hung their guns from the straps inside their coats, opened the door, and left as inconspicuously as they had come, just as Malcolm finished his piece of cake.

Malcolm moved slowly from office to office, floor to floor. Although his eyes saw, his mind didn't register. When he found the mangled body that had once been Tamatha, the knowledge hit him. He stared for minutes, trembling. Fear grabbed him, and he thought, I've got to get out of here. He started running. He went all the way to the first floor before his mind took over and brought him to a halt.

Obviously they've gone, he thought, or I'd be dead now. Who "they" were never entered his mind. He suddenly realized his vulnerability. My God, he thought, I have no gun, I couldn't even fight them if they came back. Malcolm looked at Walter's body and the heavy automatic strapped to the dead man's belt. Blood covered the gun. Malcolm couldn't bring himself to touch it. He ran to Walter's desk. Walter kept a very special weapon clipped in the leg space of his desk, a sawed-off 20-gauge shotgun. The weapon held only one shell, but Walter often bragged how it saved his life at Chosen Reservoir. Malcolm grabbed it by its pistol-like butt. He kept it pointed at the closed door as he slowly sidestepped toward Mrs. Russell's desk. Walter kept a revolver in her drawer, "just in case." Mrs. Russell, a widow, had called it her "rape gun." "Not to fight them off," she would say, "but to encourage them." Malcolm stuck the gun in his belt, then picked up the phone.

Dead. He punched all the lines. Nothing.

I have to leave, he thought, I have to get help. He tried to shove the shotgun under his jacket. Even sawed off, the gun was too long: the barrel stuck out through the collar and bumped his throat. Reluctantly, he put the shotgun back under Walter's desk, thinking he should try to leave everything as he found it. After a hard swallow, he went to the door and looked out the wide-angled peephole. The street was empty. The rain had stopped. Slowly, standing well behind the wall, he opened the door. Nothing happened. He stepped out on the stoop. Silence. With a bang he closed the door, quickly walked through the gate and down the street, his eyes darting, hunting for anything unusual. Nothing.

Malcolm headed straight for the corner phone. Each of the four divisions of the CIA has an unlisted "panic number,'' a phone number to be used only in the event of a major catastrophe, only if all other channels of communication are unavailable. Penalty for misuse of the number can be as stiff as expulsion from the service with loss of pay. Their panic number is the one top secret every CIA employee from the highest cleared director to the lowest cleared janitor knows and remembers.

The Panic Line is always manned by highly experienced agents. They have to be sharp even though they seldom do anything. When a panic call comes through, decisions must be made, quickly and correctly.

Stephen Mitchell was officer of the day manning ID's Panic phone when Malcolm's call came through. Mitchell had been one of the best traveling (as opposed to resident) agents in the CIA. For thirteen years he moved from trouble spot to trouble spot, mainly in South America. Then in 1967 a double agent in Buenos Aires planted a plastic bomb under the driver's seat in Mitchell's Simca. The double agent made an error: the explosion only blew off Mitchell's legs. The error caught the double agent in the form of a wire loop tightened in Rio. The Agency, not wanting to waste a good man, shifted Mitchell to the Panic Section.

Mitchell answered the phone after the first ring. When he picked up the receiver a tape recorder came on and a trace automatically began.

"493–7282." All CIA telephones are answered by their numbers.

"This is . . ." For a horrible second Malcolm forgot his code name. He knew he had to give his department and section number (to distinguish himself from other agents who might have the same code name), but he couldn't remember his code name. He knew better than to use his real name. Then he remembered. "This is Condor, Section 9, Department 17. We've been hit."

"Are you on an Agency line?"

"I'm calling from an open booth a little ways from . . . base. Our phones aren't working."

Shit, thought Mitchell, we have to use double talk. With his free hand he punched the Alert button. At five different locations, three in Washington, two in Langley, heavily armed men scurried to cars, turned on their engines, and waited for instructions. "How bad?"

"Maximum, total. I'm the only one who : . ."

Mitchell cut him off. "Right. Do any civilians in the area know?"

"I don't think so. Somehow it was done quietly."

"Are you damaged?"

"No."

"Are you armed?"

"Yes."

"Are there any hostiles in the area?"

Malcolm looked around. He remembered how ordinary the morning had seemed. "I don't think so, but I can't be sure."

"Listen very closely. Leave the area, slowly, but get your ass away from there, someplace safe. Wait an hour. After you're sure you're clean, call again. That will be at 1:45. Do you understand?"

"Yes."

"OK, hang up now, and remember, don't lose your head."

Mitchell broke the connection before Malcolm had taken the phone from his ear.

After Malcolm hung up, he stood on the corner for a few

seconds, trying to formulate a plan. He knew he had to find someplace safe where he could hide unnoticed for an hour, someplace close. Slowly, very slowly, he turned and walked up the street. Fifteen minutes later he joined the Iowa City Jaycees on their tour of the nation's Capitol building.

Even as Malcolm spoke to Mitchell, one of the largest and most intricate government machines in the world began to grind. Assistants monitoring Malcolm's call dispatched four cars from Washington security posts and one car from Langley with a mobile medical team, all bound for Section 9, Department 17. The squad leaders were briefed and established procedure via radio as they homed in on the target. The proper Washington police precinct was alerted to the possibility of an assistance request by "federal enforcement officials." By the time Malcolm hung up, all D.C. area CIA bases had received a hostile-action report. They activated special security plans. Within three minutes of the call all deputy directors were notified, and within six minutes the director, who had been in conference with the Vice-President, was personally briefed over a scrambled phone by Mitchell. Within eight minutes all the other main organs of America's intelligence community received news of a possible hostile action.

In the meantime Mitchell ordered all files pertaining to the Society sent to his office. During a panic situation, the Panic officer of the day automatically assumes awesome power. He virtually runs much of the entire Agency until personally relieved by a deputy director. Only seconds after Mitchell ordered the files, Records called him back.

"Sir, the computer check shows all primary files on Section 9, Department 17, are missing."

"They're *what?*"

"Missing, sir."

"Then send me the secondary set, and God damn it, send it under guard!" Mitchell slammed the phone down before the startled clerk could reply. Mitchell grabbed another phone and connected immediately. "Freeze the base," he ordered. Within seconds all exits from the compound were sealed. Anyone attempting to leave or enter the area would have been shot. Red lights flashed throughout the buildings. Special security teams began clearing the corridors, ordering all those not engaged in Panic or Red priority business to return to their base offices. Reluctance or even hesitance to comply with the order meant a gun barrel in the stomach and handcuffs on the wrists.

The door to the Panic Room opened just after Mitchell froze the base. A large man strode firmly past the security guard without bothering to return the cursory salute. Mitchell was still on the phone, so the man settled down in a chair next to the second in command.

"What the hell is going on?" The man would normally have been answered without question, but right now Mitchell was God. The second looked at his chief. Mitchell, though still barking orders into the phone, heard the demand. He nodded to his second, who in turn gave the big man a complete synopsis of what had happened and what had been done. By the time the second had finished, Mitchell was off the phone, using a soiled handkerchief to wipe his brow.

The big man stirred in his chair. "Mitchell," he said, "if it's all right with you, I think I'll stay around and give you a hand. After all, I am head of Department 17."

"Thank you, sir," Mitchell replied, "I'll be glad of any help you can give us."

The big man grunted and settled down to wait.

* * *

If you had been walking down Southeast A just behind the Library of Congress at 1:09 on that cloudy Thursday afternoon, you would have been startled by a sudden flurry of activity. Half a dozen men sprang out of nowhere and converged on a three-story white building. Just before they reached the door, two cars, one on each side of the road, double-parked almost in front of the building. A man sat in the back seat of each car, peering intently at the building and cradling something in his arms. The six men on foot went through the gate together, but only one climbed the steps. He fiddled with a large ring of keys and the lock. When the door clicked, he nodded to the others. After throwing the door wide open and hesitating for an instant, the six men poured inside, slamming the door behind them. A man got out of each car. They slowly began to pace up and down in front of the building. As the cars pulled away to park, the drivers both nodded at men standing on the corners.

Three minutes later the door opened. A man left the building and walked slowly toward the closest parked car. Once inside, he picked up a phone. Within seconds he was talking to Mitchell.

"They were hit all right, hard." The man speaking was Allan Newberry. He had seen combat in Vietnam, at the Bay of Pigs, in the mountains of Turkey, dozens of alleys, dark buildings, and basements all over the world, yet Mitchell could feel uneasy sickness in the clipped voice.

"How and how bad?" Mitchell was just beginning to believe.

"Probably a two- to five-man team, no sign of forcible entry. They must have used silenced machine guns of some sort or the whole town would have heard. Six dead in the building, four men, two women. Most of them probably didn't know what hit them. No signs of an extensive search, security camera and film destroyed. Phones are dead, probably cut somewhere. A couple of bodies will have to be worked on before identity can be definitely established. Neat, clean, and quick. They knew what they were doing down to the last detail, and they knew how to do it.''

Mitchell waited until he was sure Newberry had finished. ''OK. This is beyond me. I'm going to hold definite action until somebody upstairs orders it. Meantime you and your men sit tight. Nothing is to be moved. I want that place frozen and sealed but good. Use whatever means you must.''

Mitchell paused, both to emphasize his meaning and to hope he wasn't making a mistake. He had just authorized Newberry's team to do anything, including premeditated, nondefensive kills, Stateside action without prior clearance. Murder by whim, if they thought the whim might mean something. The consequences of such a rare order could be very grave for all concerned. Mitchell continued. ''I'm sending out more men to cover the neighborhood as additional security. I'll also send out a crime lab team, but they can only do things that won't disturb the scene. They'll bring a communications setup, too. Understand?''

''I understand. Oh, there's something a little peculiar we've found.''

Mitchell said, ''Yes?''

''Our radio briefing said there was only one door. We found two. Make any sense to you?''

''None,'' said Mitchell, ''but nothing about this whole thing makes sense. Is there anything else?''

"Just one thing." The voice grew colder. "Some son of a bitch butchered a little girl on the third floor. He didn't hit her, he butchered her." Newberry signed off.

"What now?" asked the big man.

"We wait," said Mitchell, leaning back in his wheel-chair. "We sit and wait for Condor to call."

At 1:40 Malcolm found a phone booth in the Capitol. With change acquired from a bubbly teen-age girl he dialed the panic number. It didn't even finish one complete ring.

"493–7282." The voice on the phone was tense.

"This is Condor, Section 9, Department 17. I'm in a public phone booth, I don't think I was followed, and I'm pretty sure I can't be heard."

"You've been confirmed. We've got to get you to Lang-ley, but we're afraid to let you come in solo. Do you know the Circus 3 theaters in the Georgetown district?"

"Yes."

"Could you be there in an hour?"

"Yes."

"OK. Now, who do you know at least by sight who's stationed at Langley?"

Malcolm thought for a moment. "I had an instructor code-named Sparrow IV."

"Hold on." Through priority use of the computer and communications facilities, Mitchell verified Sparrow IV's existence and determined that he was in the building. Two minutes later he said, "OK, this is what is going to happen. Half an hour from now Sparrow IV and one other man will park in a small alley behind the theaters. They'll wait exactly one hour. That gives you thirty minutes leeway either direction. There are three entrances to the alley you can take on foot. All three allow you to see anybody in front of you before they see you. When you're sure you're clean, go down the alley. If you see anything or anybody suspicious, if Sparrow IV and his partner aren't there or somebody is with them, if a God damn pigeon is at their feet, get your ass out of there, find someplace safe, and call in. Do the same if you can't make it. OK?''

"OKahahaachoo!''

Mitchell almost shot out of his wheelchair. "What the hell was that? Are you OK?''

Malcolm wiped the phone off. "Yes, sir, I'm fine. Sorry, I have a cold. I know what to do.''

"For the love of Christ.'' Mitchell hung up. He leaned back in his chair. Before he could say anything, the big man spoke.

"Look here, Mitchell. If you have no objection, I'll accompany Sparrow IV. The Department is my responsibility, and there's no young tough around here who can carry off what might be a tricky situation any better, tired old man as I may be.''

Mitchell looked at the big, confident man across from him, then smiled. "OK. Pick up Sparrow IV at the gate. Use your car. Have you ever met Condor?''

The big man shook his head. "No, but I think I've seen him. Can you supply a photo?''

Mitchell nodded and said, "Sparrow IV has one. Ordnance will give you anything you want, thought I suggest a hand gun. Any preference?''

The big man walked toward the door. "Yes,'' he said, looking back, "a .38 Special with silencer just in case we have to move quietly.''

"It'll be waiting in the car, complete with ammo. Oh,''

said Mitchell, stopping the big man as he was halfway out the door, "thanks again, Colonel Weatherby."

The big man turned and smiled. "Think nothing of it, Mitchell. After all, it's my job." He closed the door behind him and walked toward his car. After a few steps he began to wheeze very softly.

"Faulty execution of a winning combination has lost many a game on the very brink of victory. In such cases a player sees the winning idea, plays the winning sacrifice and then inverts the order of his follow-up moves or misses the really clinching point of his combination."

—Fred Reinfeld, The Complete Chess Course

Thursday Afternoon

Malcolm had little trouble finding a taxi, considering the weather. Twenty minutes later he paid the driver two blocks from the Circus theaters. Again he knew it was all-important that he stay out of sight. A few minutes later he sat at a table in the darkest corner of a bar crowded with men. The bar Malcolm chose is the most active male homosexual hangout in Washington. Starting with the early lunch hour at eleven and running until well after midnight, men of all ages, usually middle to upper middle class, fill the bar to find a small degree of relaxation among their own kind. It's a happy as well as a "gay" bar. Rock music blares, laughter drifts into the street. The levity is strained, heavy with irony, but it's there.

Malcolm hoped he looked inconspicuous, one man in a bar crowded with men. He nursed his tequila Collins, drinking it as slowly as he dared, watching faces in the crowd for signs of recognition. Some of the faces in the crowd watched him too.

No one in the bar noticed that only Malcolm's left hand rested on the small table. Under the table his right hand held a gun, a gun he pointed at anyone coming near him.

At 2:40 Malcolm jumped from his table to join a large group leaving the bar. Once outside, he quickly walked away from the group. For several minutes he crossed and recrossed Georgetown's narrow streets, carefully watching the people around him. At three o'clock, satisfied he was clean, he headed toward the Circus theaters.

Sparrow IV turned out to be a shaky, spectacled instructor of governmental procedure. He had been given no choice concerning his role in the adventure. He made it quite clear that this was not what he was hired for, he most definitely objected, and he was very concerned about his wife and four children. Mostly to shut him up, Ordnance dressed him in a bulletproof vest. He wore the hot and heavy armor under his shirt. The canvas frustrated his scratching attempts. He had no recollection of anyone called Condor or Malcolm; he lectured Junior Officer Training classes by the dozen. The people at Ordnance didn't care, but they listened anyway.

Weatherby briefed the drivers of the crash cars as they walked toward the parking lot. He checked the short gun with the sausage-shaped device and nodded his approval to the somber man from Ordnance. Ordinarily Weatherby would have had to sign for the gun, but Mitchell's authority rendered such procedures unnecessary. The Ordnance man helped Weatherby adjust a special shoulder holster, handed him twenty-five extra rounds, and wished him luck. Weatherby grunted as he climbed into his light blue sedan.

The three cars rolled out of Langley in close formation with Weatherby's blue sedan in the middle position. Just as they exited from the Beltway turnpike to enter Washington, the rear car "blew" a tire. The driver "lost control" of his vehicle, and the car ended up across two lanes of traffic. No one was hurt, but the accident blocked traffic for ten minutes. Weatherby closely followed the other crash car as it turned and twisted its way through the maze of Washington traffic. On a quiet residential street in the city's southwest quadrant the crash car made a complete U-turn and started back in the opposite direction. As it passed the blue sedan, the driver flashed Weatherby the OK sign, then sped out of sight. Weatherby headed toward Georgetown, checking for tails all the way.

Weatherby figured out his mistake. When he dispatched the assassination team, he ordered them to kill everyone in the building. He had said everyone, but he hadn't specified how many that was. His men had followed orders, but the orders hadn't been complete enough to let them know one man was missing. Why the man wasn't there Weatherby didn't know and he didn't care. If he had known about the missing man, this Condor, he could have arranged a satisfactory solution. He had made the mistake, so now he had to rectify it.

There was a chance Condor was harmless, that he wouldn't remember his conversation with the Heidegger man, but Weatherby couldn't take that chance. Heidegger questioned all the staff except Dr. Lappe. Those questions could not be allowed to exist. Now one man knew about those questions, so, like the others, that man must die even if he didn't realize what he knew.

Weatherby's plan was simple, but extremely dangerous. As soon as Condor appeared he would shoot him. Self-defense. Weatherby glanced at the trembling Sparrow IV. An unavoidable side product. The big man had no qualms concerning the instructor's pending death. The plan was fraught with risks: Condor might be better with his weapon than anticipated, the scene might be witnessed and later reported, the Agency might not believe his story and use a guaranteed form of interrogation, Condor might turn himself in some other way. A hundred things could go wrong. But no matter how high the risks, Weatherby knew they were not the certainty that faced him should he fail. He might be able to escape the Agency and the rest of the American intelligence network. There are several ways, ways that have been successfully used before. Such things were Weatherby's forte. But he knew he would never escape the striking-looking man with strange eyes. That man never failed when he acted directly. Never. He would act directly against Weatherby the dangerous bungler, Weatherby the threat. This Weatherby knew, and it made him wheeze painfully. It was this knowledge that made any thought of escape or betrayal absurd. Weatherby had to account for his error. Condor had to die.

Weatherby drove through the alley slowly, then turned around and came back, parking the car next to some garbage cans behind the theaters. The alley was empty just as Mitchell said it would be. Weatherby doubted if anyone would enter it while they were there: Washingtonians tend to avoid alleys. He knew Mitchell would arrange for the area to be free of police so that uniforms wouldn't frighten Condor. That was fine with Weatherby. He motioned for Sparrow IV to get out. They leaned against the car, prominent and visibly alone. Then, like any good hunter staging an ambush, Weatherby blanked his mind to let his senses concentrate.

Malcolm saw them standing there before they knew he was in the alley. He watched them very carefully from a distance of about sixty paces. He had a hard time controlling sneezes, but he managed to stay silent. After he was certain they were alone, he stepped from behind the telephone pole and began to walk toward them. His relief built with every step.

Weatherby spotted Malcolm immediately. He stepped away from the car, ready. He wanted to be very, very sure, and sixty paces is only a fair shot for a silenced pistol. He also wanted to be out of Sparrow IV's reach. Take them one at a time, he thought.

Recognition sprang on Malcolm twenty-five paces from the two men, five paces sooner than Weatherby anticipated any action. A picture of a man in a blue sedan parked just up from the Society in the morning rain flashed through Malcolm's mind. The man in that car and one of the men now standing in front of him were the same. Something was wrong, something was very wrong. Malcolm stopped, then slowly backed up. Almost unconsciously he tugged at the gun in his belt.

Weatherby knew something was wrong, too. His quarry had quite unexpectedly stopped short of the trap, was now fleeing, and was probably preparing an aggressive defense. Malcolm's unexpected actions forced Weatherby to abandon his original plan and react to a new situation. While he quickly drew his own weapon, Weatherby briefly noted Sparrow IV, frozen with fright and bewilderment. The timid instructor still posed no threat.

Weatherby was a veteran of many situations requiring rapid action. Malcolm's pistol barrel had just cleared his belt when Weatherby fired.

A pistol, while effective, can be a difficult weapon to use under field conditions, even for an experienced veteran. A pistol equipped with a silencer increases this difficulty, for while the silencer allows the handler to operate quietly, it cuts down on his efficiency. The bulk at the end of the barrel is an unaccustomed weight requiring aim compensation by the user. Ballistically, a silencer cuts down on the bullet's velocity. The silencer may affect the bullet's trajectory. A silencer-equipped pistol is cumbersome, difficult to draw and fire quickly.

All these factors worked against Weatherby. Had he not been using a silenced pistol—even though his quarry's retreat forced him to take time to revise his plans—there would have been no contest. As it was, the pistol's bulk slowed his draw. He lost accuracy attempting to regain speed. The veteran killer tried for the difficult but definite head shot, but he overcompensated. Milliseconds after the soft *plop!*, a heavy chunk of lead cut through the hair hanging over Malcolm's left ear and whined off to sink in the Potomac.

Malcolm had only fired one pistol in his life, a friend's .22 target model. All five shots missed the running gopher. He fired Mrs. Russell's gun from the waist, and a deafening roar echoed down the alley before he knew he had pulled the trigger.

When a man is shot with a .357 magnum he doesn't grab

a neat little red hole in his body and slide slowly to the ground. He goes down hard. At twenty-five paces the effect is akin to being hit by a truck. Malcolm's bullet smashed through Weatherby's left thigh. The force of the blast splattered a large portion of Weatherby's leg over the alley; it flipped him into the air and slammed him face down in the road.

Sparrow IV looked incredulously at Malcolm. Slowly Malcolm turned toward the little instructor, bringing the gun into line with the man's quivering stomach.

"He was one of them!" Malcolm was panting though he hadn't exerted himself. "He was one of them!" Malcolm slowly backed away from the speechless instructor. When he reached the edge of the alley, Malcolm turned and ran.

Weatherby groaned, fighting off the shock of the wound. The pain hadn't set in. He was a very tough man, but it took everything he had to raise his arm. He had somehow held on to the gun. Miraculously, his mind stayed clear. Very carefully he aimed and fired. Another *plop!*, and a bullet shattered on the theater wall, but not before it tore through the throat of Sparrow IV, instructor of governmental procedure, husband, father of four. As the body crumpled against the car, Weatherby felt a strange sense of elation. He wasn't dead yet, Condor had vanished again, and there would be no bullets for Ballistics to use in determining who shot whom. There was still hope. He passed out.

A police car found the two men. It took them a long time to respond to the frightened shopkeeper's call, because all the Georgetown units had been sent to check out a sniper report. The report turned out to be from a crank.

* * *

Malcolm ran four blocks before he realized how conspicuous he was. He slowed down, turned several corners, then hailed a passing taxi to downtown Washington.

Sweet Jesus, Malcolm thought, he was one of them. He was one of them. The Agency must not have known. He had to get to a phone. He had to call . . . Fear set in. Suppose, just suppose the man in the alley wasn't the only double. Suppose he had been sent there by a man who knew what he was. Suppose the man at the other end of the Panic Line was also a double.

Malcolm quit his suppositions to deal with the immediate problem of survival. Until he thought it out he wouldn't dare call in. And they would be looking for him. They would have looked for him even before the shooting, the only survivor of the section, they. . . But he wasn't! The thought raced through his mind. He wasn't the only survivor of the section. Heidegger! Heidegger was sick, home in bed, sick! Malcolm searched his brain. Address, what did Heidegger say his address was? Malcolm had heard Heidegger tell Dr. Lappe his address was . . . Mount Royal Arms!

Malcolm explained his problem to the cabby. He was on his way to pick up a blind date, but he had forgotten the address. All he knew was she lived in the Mount Royal Arms. The cabby, always eager to help young love, called his dispatcher, who gave him the address in the northwest quadrant. When the cabby let him out in front of the aging building, Malcolm gave him a dollar tip.

Heidegger's name tape was stuck next to 413. Malcolm buzzed. No return buzz, no query over the call box. While he buzzed again, an uneasy but logical assumption grew in his mind. Finally he pushed three other buzzers. No answer came, so he punched a whole row. When the jammed call box squealed, he yelled, "Special delivery!" The door buzzer rang and he ran inside.

No one answered his knock at Apartment 413, but by then he didn't really expect an answer. He got on his knees and looked at the lock. If he was right, only a simple spring night lock was on. In dozens of books he'd read and in countless movies, the hero uses a small piece of stiff plastic and in a few seconds a locked door springs open. Plastic—where could he find a piece of stiff plastic? After several moments of frantic pocket slapping, he opened his wallet and removed his laminated CIA identification card. The card certified he was an employee of Tentrex Industries, Inc., giving relevant information regarding his appearance and identity. Malcolm had always liked the two photos of himself, one profile, one full face.

For twenty minutes Malcolm sneezed, grunted, pushed, pulled, jiggled, pleaded, threatened, shook, and finally hacked at the lock with his card. The plastic lamination finally split, shooting his ID card through the crack and into the locked room.

Frustration turned to anger. Malcolm relieved his cramped knees by standing. If nobody has bothered me up till now, he thought, a little more noise won't make much difference. Backed with the fury, fear, and frustration of the day, Malcolm smashed his foot against the door. Locks and doors in the Mount Royal Arms are not of the finest quality. The management leans toward cheap rent, and the building construction is similarly inclined. The door of 413 flew inward, bounced off its doorstop, and was caught on the return swing by Malcolm. He shut the door a good deal more quietly than he had opened it. He picked his ID card out of the splinters, then crossed the room to the bed and what lay on it.

Since time forestalled any pretense, they hadn't bothered to be gentle with Heidegger. If Malcolm had lifted the pajama top, he would have seen the mark a low-line punch leaves if the victim's natural tendency to bruise is arrested by death. The corpse's face was blackish blue, a state induced by, among other things, strangulation. The room stank from the corpse's involuntary discharge.

Malcolm looked at the beginning-to-bloat body. He knew very little about organic medicine, but he knew that this state of decomposition is not reached in a couple of hours. Therefore Heidegger had been killed before the others. "They" hadn't come here after they discovered him missing from work but before they hit the building. Malcolm didn't understand.

Heidegger's right pajama sleeve lay on the floor. Malcolm didn't think that type of tear would be made in a fight. He flipped the covers back to look at Heidegger's arm. On the underside of the forearm he found a small bruise, the kind a tiny bug would make. Or, thought Malcolm, remembering his trips to the student health service, a clumsily inserted hypodermic. They shot him full of something, probably to make him talk. About what? Malcolm had no idea. He began to search the room when he remembered about fingerprints. Taking his handkerchief from his pocket, he wiped everything he remembered touching, including the outside of the door. He found a pair of dusty handball gloves on the cluttered dresser. Too small, but they covered his fingers.

After the bureau drawers he searched the closet. On the top shelf he found an envelope full of money, fifty- and one-hundred-dollar bills. He didn't take the time to count it, but he estimated that there must be at least ten thousand dollars.

He sat on the clothes-covered chair. It didn't make sense. An ex-alcoholic, an accountant who lectured on the merits of mutual funds, a man frightened of muggers, keeping all that cash stashed in his closet. It didn't make sense. He looked at the corpse. At any rate, he thought, Heidegger won't need it now. Malcolm put the envelope inside his shorts. After a last quick look around, he cautiously opened the door, walked down the stairs, and caught a downtown bus at the corner.

Malcolm knew his first problem would be evading his pursuers. By now there would be at least two "they"s after him: the Agency and whatever group hit the Society. They all knew what he looked like, so his first move would have to be to change his appearance.

The sign in the barbershop said "No Waiting," and for once advertising accurately reflected its product. Malcolm took off his jacket facing the wall. He slipped the gun inside the bundle before he sat down. His eyes never left the jacket during the whole haircut.

"What do you want, young fellow?" The graying barber snipped his scissors gleefully.

Malcolm felt no regrets. He knew how much the haircut might mean. "A short butch, just a little longer than a crew cut, long enough so it will lay down."

"Say, that'll be quite a change." The barber plugged in an electric clipper.

"Yeah."

"Say, young man, are you interested in baseball? I sure

am. I read an article in the *Post* today about the Orioles and spring training, and the way this fellow figures it . . ."

After the haircut Malcolm looked in the mirror. He hadn't seen that person for five years.

His next stop was Sunny's Surplus. Malcolm knew a good disguise starts with the right attitude, but he also knew good props were invaluable. He searched through the entire stock until he found a used field jacket with the patches intact that fitted reasonably well. The name patch above the left pocket read "Evans." On the left shoulder was a tricolored eagle patch with the word "Airborne" in gold letters on a black background. Malcolm knew he had just become a veteran of the 101st Airborne Division. He bought and changed into a pair of blue stretch jeans and an outrageously priced set of used jump boots ("$15, guaranteed to have seen action in Vietnam"). He also bought underwear, a cheap pullover, black driving gloves, socks, a safety razor, and a toothbrush. When he left the store with his bundle under his arm, he pretended he had a spike rammed up his ass. His steps were firm and well measured. He looked cockily at every girl he passed. After five blocks he needed a rest, so he entered one of Washington's countless Hot Shoppe restaurants.

"Can Ah have a cup of caufee?" The waitress didn't bat an eye at Malcolm's newly acquired southern accent. She brought him his coffee. Malcolm tried to relax and think.

Two girls were in the booth behind Malcolm. A lifetime habit made him listen to their conversation.

"So you're not going anywhere for your vacation?"

"No, I'm just going to stay home. For two weeks I'll shut the world out."

"You'll go crazy."

"Maybe, but don't try calling me for a progress report, because I probably won't even answer the phone."

The other girl laughed. "What if it's a hunk of man who's just pining for companionship?"

The other girl snorted. "Then he'll just have to wait for two weeks. I'm going to relax."

"Well, it's your life. Sure you won't have dinner tonight?"

"No, really, thanks, Anne. I'm just going to finish my coffee and then drive home, and starting right now I won't have to hurry for another two weeks."

"Well, Wendy, have fun." Thighs squeaked across plastic. The girl called Anne walked toward the door, right past Malcolm. He caught a glimpse of a tremendous pair of legs, blond hair, and a firm profile vanishing in the crowd. He sat very still, sniffling occasionally, nervous as hell, for he had found the answer to his shelter problem.

It took the girl called Wendy five minutes to finish her coffee. When she left she didn't even look at the man sitting behind her. She couldn't have seen much anyway, as his face was hidden behind a menu. Malcolm followed her as soon as she paid and started out the door. He threw his money on the counter as he left.

All he could tell from behind was that she was tall, thin but not painfully skinny like Tamatha, had short black hair, and only medium legs. Christ, he thought, why couldn't she have been the blond? Malcolm's luck held, for the girl's car was in the back section of a crowded parking lot. He casually followed her past the fat attendant leering from behind a battered felt hat. Just as the girl unlocked the door of a battered Corvair, Malcolm yelled, "Wendy! My God, what are you doing here?"

Startled, but not alarmed, the girl looked up at the smiling figure in the army jacket walking toward her.

"Are you talking to me?" She had narrow-set brown eyes, a wide mouth, a little nose, and high cheekbones. A perfectly ordinary face. She wore little or no makeup.

"I shore am. Don't you remember me, Wendy?" He was only three steps from her now.

"I . . . I don't think so." She noticed that his one hand held a package and his other was inside his jacket.

Malcolm stood beside her now. He set the package on the roof of her car and casually placed his left hand behind her head. He tightly grabbed her neck, bending her head down until she saw the gun in his other hand.

"Don't scream or make any quick moves or I'll splatter you all over the street. Understand?" Malcolm felt the girl shiver, but she nodded quickly. "Now get in the car and unlock the other door. This thing shoots through windows and I won't even hesitate." The girl quickly climbed into the driver's seat, leaned over, and unlocked the other door. Malcolm slammed her door shut, picked up his package, slowly walked around the car, and got in.

"Please don't hurt me." Her voice was much softer than in the restaurant.

"Look at me." Malcolm had to clear his throat. "I'm not going to hurt you, not if you do exactly as I say. I don't want your money, I don't want to rape you. But you must do exactly as I say. Where do you live?"

"In Alexandria."

"We're going to your apartment. You'll drive. If you have any ideas about signaling for help, forget them. If you try, I'll shoot. I might get hurt, but you'll be dead. It's not worth it. OK?" The girl nodded. "Let's go."

The drive to Virginia was tense. Malcolm never took his eyes off the girl. She never took her eyes off the road. Just after the Alexandria exit she pulled into a small courtyard surrounded by apartment units.

"Which one is yours?"

"The first one. I have the top two floors. A man lives in the basement."

"You're doing just fine. Now, when we go up the walk, just pretend you're taking a friend to your place. Remember, I'm right behind you."

They got out and walked the few steps to the building. The girl shook and had trouble unlocking the door, but she finally made it. Malcolm followed her in, gently closing the door behind him.

"I have treated this game in great detail because I think it is important for the student to see what he's up against, and how he ought to go about solving the problems of practical play. You may not be able to play the defense and counterattack this well, but the game sets a worthwhile goal for you to achieve: how to fight back in a position where your opponent has greater mobility and better prospects."

—Fred Reinfeld, *The Complete Chess Course*

Thursday Evening– Friday Morning

"I don't believe you." The girl sat on the couch, her eyes glued to Malcolm. She was not as frightened as she had been, but her heart felt as if it was breaking ribs.

Malcolm sighed. He had been sitting across from the girl for an hour. From what he found in her purse, he knew she was Wendy Ross, twenty-seven years old, had lived and driven in Carbondale, Illinois, distributed 135 pounds on her five-foot-ten frame (he was sure that was an overestimated lie), regularly gave Type O Positive blood to the Red Cross, was a card-carrying user of the Alexandria Public Library and a member of the University of Southern Illinois Alumni Association, and was certified to receive and deliver summonses for her employers, Bechtel, Barber, Sievers, Holloron, and Muckleston. From what he read on her face, he knew she was frightened and telling the truth when she said she didn't believe him. Malcolm didn't blame her, as he really didn't believe his story either, and he knew it was true.

"Look," he said, "if what I said wasn't true, why would I try to convince you it was?"

"I don't know."

"Oh, Jesus!" Malcolm paced the room. He could tie her up and still use her place, but that was risky. Besides, she could be invaluable. He had an inspiration in the middle of a sneeze.

"Look," he said, wiping his upper lip, "suppose I could at least prove to you I was with the CIA. Then would you believe me?"

"I might." A new look crossed the girl's face.

"OK, look at this." Malcolm sat down beside her. He felt her body tense, but she took the mutilated piece of paper.

"What's this?"

"It's my CIA identification card. See, that's me with long hair."

Her voice was cold. "It says Tentrex Industries, not CIA. I can read, you know." He could see she regretted her inflection after she said it, but she didn't apologize.

"I know what it says!" Malcolm grew more impatient and nervous. His plan might not work. "Do you have a D.C. phone book?"

The girl nodded toward an end table. Malcolm crossed the room, picked up the huge book, and flung it at the girl. Her reactions were so keyed she caught it without any trouble. Malcolm shouted at her, "Look in there for Tentrex Industries. Anywhere! White pages, yellow pages, anywhere. The card gives a phone number and an address on Wisconsin Avenue, so it should be in the book. Look!"

The girl looked, then she looked again. She closed the book and stared at Malcolm. "So you've got an ID card for a place that doesn't exist. What does that prove?"

"Right!" Malcolm crossed the room excitedly, bringing the phone with him. The cord barely reached. "Now," he said, very secretively, "look up the Washington number for the Central Intelligence Agency. The numbers are the same."

The girl opened the book again and turned the pages. For a long time she sat puzzled, then with a new look and a questioning voice she said, "Maybe you checked this out before you made the card, just for times like this."

Shit, thought Malcolm. He let all the air out of his lungs, took a deep breath, and started again. "OK, maybe I did, but there's one way to find out. Call that number."

"It's after five," said the girl. "If no one answers am I supposed to believe you until morning?"

Patiently, calmly, Malcolm explained to her. "You're right. If Tentrex is a real company, it's closed for the day. But CIA doesn't close. Call that number and ask for

Tentrex.'' He handed her the phone. "One thing. I'll be listening, so don't do anything wrong. Hang up when I tell you."

The girl nodded and made the call. Three rings.

"WE4–3926."

"May I have Tentrex Industries, please?" The girl's voice was very dry.

"I'm sorry," said a soft voice. A faint click came over the line. "Everyone at Tentrex has gone for the day. They'll be back in the morning. May I ask who is calling and what the nature of your business . . ."

Malcolm broke the connection before the trace had a chance to even get a general fix. The girl slowly replaced the receiver. For the first time she looked directly at Malcolm. "I don't know if I believe everything you say," she said, "but I think I believe some of it."

"One final piece of proof." Malcolm took the gun out of his pants and laid it carefully in her lap. He walked across the room and sat in the beanbag chair. His palms were damp, but it was better to take the risk now than later. "You've got the gun. You could shoot me at least once before I got to you. There's the phone. I believe in you enough to think you believe me. Call anybody you want. Police, CIA, FBI, I don't care. Tell them you've got me. But I want you to know what might happen if you do. The wrong people might get the call. They might get here first. If they do, we're both dead."

For a long time the girl sat still, looking at the heavy gun in her lap. Then, in a soft voice Malcolm had to strain to hear, she said, "I believe you."

She suddenly burst into activity. She stood up, laid the gun on the table and paced the room. "I . . . I don't know what I can do to help you, but I'll try. You can stay here in the extra bedroom. Umm." She looked toward the small kitchen and meekly said, "I could make something to eat."

Malcolm grinned, a genuine smile he thought he had lost. "That would be wonderful. Could you do one thing for me?"

"Anything, anything, I'll do anything." Wendy's nerves unwound as she realized she might live.

"Could I use your shower? The hair down my back is killing me."

She grinned at him and they both laughed. She showed him the bathroom upstairs and provided him with soap, shampoo, and towels. She didn't say a word when he took the gun with him. As soon as she left him he tiptoed to the top of the stairs. No sound of a door opening, no telephone dialing. When he heard drawers opening and closing, silverware rattling, he went back to the bathroom, undressed, and climbed into the shower.

Malcolm stayed in the shower for thirty minutes, letting the soft pellets of water drive freshness through his body. The steam cleared his sinuses, and by the time he shut off the water he felt almost human. He changed into his new pullover and fresh underwear. He automatically looked in the mirror to straighten his hair. It was so short he did it with two strokes of his hand.

The stereo was playing as he came down the stairs. He recognized the album as Vince Guaraldi's score for *Black Orpheus*. The song was "Cast Your Fate to the Wind." He had the album too, and told her so as they sat down to eat.

During green salad she told Malcolm about small-town life in Illinois. Between bites of frozen German beans he heard about life at Southern Illinois University. Mashed potatoes were mixed with a story concerning an almost financé. Between chunks of the jiffy-cooked Swiss steak he learned how drab it is to be a legal secretary for a stodgy corporate law firm in Washington. There was a lull for Sara Lee cherry-covered cheesecake. As she poured coffee she summed it all up with, "It's really been pretty dull. Up till now, of course."

During dishes he told her why he hated his first name. She promised never to use it. She threw a handful of suds at him, but quickly wiped them off.

After dishes he said good night and trudged up the stairs to the bathroom. He put his contact lenses in his portable carrying case (what I wouldn't give for my glasses and soaking case, he thought). He brushed his teeth, crossed the hall to a freshly made bed, stuck a precautionary handkerchief under his pillow, laid the gun on the night stand, and went to sleep.

She came to him shortly after midnight. At first he thought he was dreaming, but her heavy breathing and the heat from her body were too real. His first fully awake thought noted that she had just showered. He could faintly smell bath powder mingling with the sweet odor of sex. He rolled on his side, pulling her eager body against him. They found each other's mouth. Her tongue pushed through his lips, searching. She was tremendously excited. He had a hard time untangling himself from her arms so he could strip off his underwear. By now their faces were wet from each other. Naked at last, he rolled her over on her back, pulling his hand slowly up the inside of her thigh, delicately trailing his fingers across rhythmically flowing hips, up across her flat, heaving stomach to her large, erect nipples. His fingers closed on one small breast, easily gathering the mound of flesh into his hand. From out of nowhere he thought of the girl who walked past the Society's building: she had such fine, large breasts. He softly squeezed his hand. Wendy groaned loudly and pulled his head to her chest, his lips to her straining nipples. As his mouth slowly caressed her breasts, he ran his hand down, down to the wet fire between her legs. When he touched her she sucked in air, softly but firmly arching her back. She found him, and a second later softly moaned, "Now, please now!" He mounted her, clumsily as first-time lovers do. They pressed together. She tried to cover every inch of her body with him. His hard thrusts spread fire through her body. She ran her hands down his back, and just before they exploded he felt her fingernails digging into his buttocks, pulling him ever deeper.

They lay quietly together for half an hour, then they began again, slowly and more carefully, but with a greater intensity. Afterwards, as she lay cradled on his chest, she spoke. "You don't have to love me. I don't love you, I don't think so anyway. But I want you, and I need you."

Malcolm said nothing, but he drew her closer. They slept.

Other people didn't get to bed that night. When Langley heard the reports of the Weatherby shooting, already frazzled nerves frazzled more. Crash cars full of very determined men beat the ambulance to the alley. Washington police complained to their superiors about "unidentified men claiming to be federal officers" questioning witnesses. A clash between two branches of government was averted by the entrance of a third. Three more official-looking cars pulled into the neighborhood. Two very serious men in pressed white shirts and dark suits pushed their way through the milling crowd to inform commanders of the other departments that the FBI was now officially in charge. The "unidentified federal officers" and the Washington police checked with their headquarters and both were told not to push the issue.

The FBI entered the case when the powers-that-were adopted a working assumption of espionage. The National Security Act of 1947 states, "The agency [CIA] shall have no police, subpoena, law-enforcement powers, or internal security functions." The events of the day most definitely fell under the heading of internal subversive activities, activities that are the domain of the FBI. Mitchell held off informing the sister agency of details for as long as he dared, but eventually a deputy director yielded to pressure.

But the CIA would not be denied the right to investigate assaults on its agents, no matter where the assaults occurred. The Agency has a loophole through which many questionable activities funnel. The loophole, Section 5 of the Act, allows the Agency to perform "such other functions and duties related to intelligence affecting the national security as the National Security Council may from time to time direct." The Act also grants the Agency the power to question people inside the country. The directors of the Agency concluded that the extreme nature of the situation warranted direct action by the Agency. This action could and would continue until halted by a direct order from the National Security Council. In a very polite but pointed note they so informed the FBI, thanking them, of course, for their cooperation and expressing gratitude for any future help.

The Washington police were left with one corpse and a gunshot victim who had disappeared to an undisclosed hospital in Virginia, condition serious, prognosis uncertain.

They were not pleased or placated by assurances from various federal officers, but they were unable to pursue "their" case.

The jurisdictional mishmash tended to work itself out in the field, where departmental rivalry meant very little compared to dead men. The agents in charge of operations for each department agreed to coordinate their efforts. By evening one of the most extensive manhunts in Washington's history began to unfold, with Malcolm as the object of activity. By morning the hunters had turned up a good deal, but they had no clues to Malcolm's whereabouts.

This did little to brighten a bleak morning after for the men who sat around a table in a central Washington office. Most of them had been up until very late the night before, and most of them were far from happy. The liaison group included all of the CIA deputy directors and representatives from every intelligence group in the country. The man at the head of the table was the deputy director in charge of Intelligence Division. Since the crisis occurred in his division, he had been placed in charge of the investigation. He summed up the facts for the grim men he faced.

"Eight Agency people dead, one wounded, and one, a probable double, missing. Again, we have only a tentative—and I must say doubtful—explanation of why."

"What makes you think the note the killers left is a fake?" The man who spoke wore the uniform of the United States Navy.

The Deputy Director sighed. The Captain always had to have things repeated. "We're not saying it's a fake, we only think so. We think it's a ruse, an attempt to blame the Czechs for the killings. Sure, we hit one of their bases in Prague, but for tangible, valuable intelligence. We only killed one man. Now, they go in for many things, but melodramatic revenge isn't one of them. Nor is leaving notes on the scene neatly explaining everything. Especially when it gains them nothing. Nothing.''

''Ah, may I ask a question or two, Deputy?''

The Deputy leaned forward, immediately intent. ''Of course, sir.''

''Thank you.'' The man who spoke was small and delicately old. To strangers he inevitably appeared to be a kindly old uncle with a twinkle in his eye. ''Just to refresh my memory—stop me if I'm wrong—the one in the apartment, Heidegger, had sodium pentothal in his blood?''

''That's correct, sir.'' The Deputy strained, trying to remember if he had forgotten any detail in the briefing.

''Yet none of the others were 'questioned,' as far as we can tell. Very strange. They came for him in the night, before the others. Killed shortly before dawn. Yet your investigation puts our boy Malcolm at his apartment that afternoon after Weatherby was shot. You say there is nothing to indicate Heidegger was a double agent? No expenditures beyond his income, no signs of outside wealth, no reported tainted contacts, no blackmail vulnerability?''

''Nothing, sir.''

''Any signs of mental instability?'' CIA personnel are among the highest groups in the nation for incidence of mental illness.

''None, sir. Excepting his former alcoholism, he appeared to be normal, though somewhat reclusive.''

''Yes, so I read. Investigation of the others reveal anything out of the ordinary?''

''Nothing, sir.''

"Would you do me a favor and read what Weatherby said to the doctors? By the way, how is he?"

"He's doing better, sir. The doctors say he'll live, but they are taking his leg off this morning." The Deputy shuffled papers until he found the one he sought. "Here it is. Now, you must remember he has been unconscious most of the time, but once he woke up, looked at the doctors, and said, 'Malcolm shot me. He shot both of us. Get him, hit him.'"

There was a stir at the end of the table and the Navy captain leaned forward in his chair. In his heavy, slurred voice he said, "I say we find that son of a bitch and blast him out of whatever rat hole he ran into!"

The old man chuckled. "Yes. Well, I quite agree we must find our wayward Condor. But I do think it would be a pity if we 'blasted' him before he told us why he shot poor Weatherby. Indeed, why anybody was shot. Do you have anything else for us, Deputy?"

"No, sir," said the Deputy, stuffing papers into his briefcase. "I think we've covered everything. You have all the information we do. Thank you all for coming."

As the men stood to leave, the old man turned to a colleague and said quietly, "I wonder why." Then with a smile and a shake of his head he left the room.

Malcolm woke up only when Wendy's caresses became impossible for even a sick man to ignore. Her hands and mouth moved all over his body, and almost before he knew what was happening she mounted him and again he felt her fluttering warmth turn to fire. Afterwards, she looked at him for a long time, lightly touching his body as if exploring an unseen land. She touched his forehead and frowned.

"Malcolm, do you feel OK?"

Malcolm had no intention of being brave. He shook his head and forced a raspy "No" from his throat. The one word seemed to fuel the hot vise closing around his throat. Talking was out for the day.

"You're sick!" Wendy grabbed his lower jaw. "Let me see!" she ordered, and forced his mouth open. "My God, it's red down there!" She let go of Malcolm and started to climb out of bed. "I'm going to call a doctor."

Malcolm caught her arm. She turned to him with a fearful look, then smiled. "It's OK. I have a friend whose husband is a doctor. He drives by here every day on his way to a clinic in D.C. I don't think he's left yet. If he hasn't, I'll ask him to stop by to see my sick friend." She giggled. "You don't have to worry. He won't tell a soul because he'll think he's keeping another kind of secret. OK?"

Malcolm looked at her for a second, then let go of her arm and nodded. He didn't care if the doctor brought Sparrow IV's friend with him. All he wanted was relief.

The doctor turned out to be a paunchy middle-aged man who spoke little. He poked and prodded Malcolm, took his temperature, and looked down his throat so long Malcolm thought he would throw up. The doctor finally looked up and said, "You've got a mild case of strep throat, my boy." He looked at an anxious Wendy hovering nearby. "Nothing to worry about, really. We'll fix him up." Malcolm watched the doctor fiddle with something in his bag. When he turned toward Malcolm there was a hypodermic needle in his hand. "Roll over and pull your shorts down."

A picture of a limp, cold arm with a tiny puncture flashed through Malcolm's mind. He froze.

"For Christ's sake, it won't hurt that much. It's only penicillin."

After giving Malcolm his shot, the doctor turned to Wendy. "Here," he said, handing her a slip of paper. "Get this filled and see that he takes them. He'll need at least a day's rest." The doctor smiled as he leaned close to Wendy. He whispered, "And Wendy, I do mean total rest." He laughed all the way to the door. On the porch, he turned to her and slyly said, "Whom do I bill?"

Wendy smiled shyly and handed him twenty dollars. The doctor started to speak, but Wendy cut his protest short. "He can afford it. He—we—really appreciate you coming over."

"Hmph," snorted the doctor sarcastically, "he should. I'm late for my coffee break." He paused to look at her. "You know, he's the kind of prescription I've thought you needed for a long time." With a wave of his hand he was gone.

By the time Wendy got upstairs, Malcolm was asleep. She quietly left the apartment. She spent the morning shopping with the list Malcolm and she had composed while waiting for the doctor. Besides filling the prescription, she bought Malcolm several pairs of underwear, socks, some shirts and pants, a jacket, and four different paperbacks, since she didn't know what he liked to read. She carted her bundles home in time to make lunch. She spent a quiet afternoon and evening, occasionally checking on her charge. She smiled all day long.

Supervision of America's large and sometimes cumbersome intelligence community has classically posed the problem of *sed quis custodiet ipsos Custodes*: who guards the guardians? In addition to the internal checks existing independently in each agency, the National Security Act of 1947 created the National Security Council, a group whose composition varies with each change of presidential administration. The Council always includes the President and Vice-President and usually includes major cabinet members. The Council's basic duty is to oversee the activities of the intelligence agencies and to make policy decisions guiding those activities.

But the members of the National Security Council are very busy men with demanding duties besides overseeing a huge intelligence network. Council members by and large do not have the time to devote to intelligence matters, so most decisions about the intelligence community are made by a smaller Council "subcommittee" known as the Special Group. Insiders often refer to the Special Group as the "54/12 Group," so called because it was created by Secret Order 54/12 early in the Eisenhower years. The 54/12 Group is virtually unknown outside the intelligence community, and even there only a handful of men are aware of its existence.

Composition of the 54/12 Group also varies with each administration. Its membership generally includes the director of the CIA, the Under Secretary of State of Political Affairs or his deputy, and the Secretary and Deputy Secretary of Defense. In the Kennedy and early Johnson administrations the presidential representative and key man on the 54/12 Group was McGeorge Bundy. The other members were McCone, McNamara, Roswell Gilpatric (Deputy Secretary of Defense), and U. Alexis Johnson (Deputy Under Secretary of State for Political Affairs).

Overseeing the American intelligence community poses

problems for even a small, full-time group of professionals. One is that the overseers must depend on those they oversee for much of the information necessary for regulation. Such a situation is naturally a delicate perplexity.

There is also the problem of fragmented authority. For example, if an American scientist spies on the country while employed by NASA, then defects to Russia and continues his spying but does it from France, which American agency is responsible for his neutralization? The FBI, since he began his activities under their jurisdiction, or the CIA, since he shifted to activities under their purview? With the possibility of bureaucratic jealousies escalating into open rivalry, such questions take on major import.

Shortly after it was formed, the 54/12 Group tried to solve the problems of internal information and fragmented authority. The 54/12 Group established a small special security section, a section with no identity save that of staff for the 54/12 Group. The special section's duties included liaison work. The head of the special section serves on a board composed of leading staff members from all intelligence agencies. He has the power to arbitrate jurisdictional disputes. The special section also has the responsibility of independently evaluating all the information given to the 54/12 Group by the intelligence community. But most important, the special section is given the power to perform "such necessary security functions as extraordinary circumstances might dictate, subject to Group [the 54/12 Group] regulation."

To help the special section perform its duties, the 54/12 Group assigned a small staff to the section chief and allowed him to draw on other major security and intelligence groups for needed staff and authority.

The 54/12 Group knows it has created a potential problem. The special section could follow the natural tendency of most government organizations and grow in size and awkwardness, thereby becoming a part of the problem it was created to solve. The special section, small though it is, has tremendous power as well as tremendous potential. A small mistake by the section could be a lever of great magnitude. The 54/12 Group supervises its creation cautiously. They keep a firm check on any bureaucratic growth potentials in the section, they carefully review its activities, keeping the operational work of the section at a bare minimum, and they place only extraordinary men in charge of the section.

While Malcolm and Wendy waited for the doctor, a large, competent-looking man sat in an outer office on Pennsylvania Avenue, waiting to answer a very special summons. His name was Kevin Powell. He waited patiently but eagerly: he did not receive such a summons every day. Finally a secretary beckoned, and he entered the inner office of a man who looked like a kindly, delicate old uncle. The old man motioned Powell to a chair.

"Ah, Kevin, how wonderful to see you."

"Good to see you, sir. You're looking fit."

"As do you, my boy, as do you. Here." The old man tossed Powell a file folder. "Read this." As Powell read, the old man examined him closely. The plastic surgeons had done a marvelous job on his ear, and it took an experienced eye to detect the slight bulge close to his left armpit. When Powell raised his eyes, the old man said, "What do you think, my boy?"

Powell chose his words carefully. "Very strange, sir. I'm not sure what it means, though it must mean a great deal."

"Exactly my thoughts, my boy, exactly mine. Both the Agency and the Bureau [FBI] have squads of men scouring the city, watching the airports, buses, trains, the usual routine, only expanded to quite a staggering level. As you know, it's these routine operations that make or break most endeavors, and I must say they are doing fairly well. Or they were up until now."

He paused for breath and an encouraging look of interest from Powell. "They've found a barber who remembers giving our boy a haircut—rather predictable yet commendable action on his part—sometime after Weatherby was shot. By the way, he is coming along splendidly. They hope to question him late this evening. Where was I . . . Oh, yes. They canvassed the area and found where he bought some clothes, but then they lost him. They have no idea where to look next. I have one or two ideas about that myself, but I'll save them for later. There are some points I want you to check me on. See if you can answer them for me, or maybe find some questions I can't find.

"Why? Why the whole thing? If it was Czechoslovakia, why that particular branch, a do-nothing bunch of analysts? If it wasn't, we're back to our original question.

"Look at the method. Why so blatant? Why was the man Heidegger hit the night before? What did he know that the others didn't? If he was special, why kill the others too? If Malcolm works for them, they didn't need to question Heidegger about much. Malcolm could have told them.

"Then we have our boy Malcolm, Malcolm with the many 'why's.' If he is a double, why did he use the Panic procedure? If he is a double, why did he set up a meeting—to kill Sparrow IV, whom he could have picked off at his leisure had he worked at establishing the poor fellow's identity? If he isn't a double, why did he shoot the two men he called to take him to safety? Why did he go to Heidegger's apartment after the shooting? And, of course, where, why, and how is he now?

"There are a lot of other questions that grow from these, but I think these are the main ones. Do you agree?"

Powell nodded and said, "I do. Where do I fit in?"

The old man smiled. "You, my dear boy, have the good fortune to be on loan to my section. As you know, we were created to sort out the mishmashes of bureaucracy. I imagine some of those paper pushers who shuffled my poor old soul here assumed I would be stuck processing paper until I died or retired. Neither of those alternatives appeals to me, so I have redefined liaison work to mean a minimum of paper and a maximum of action, pirated a very good set of operatives, and set up my own little shop, just like in the old days. With the official maze of the intelligence community, I have a good deal of confusion to play with. A dramatist I once knew said the best way to create chaos is to flood the scene with actors. I've managed to capitalize on the chaos of others.

"I think some of my efforts," he added in a modest tone, "small though they may be, have been of some value to the country.

"Now we come to this little affair. It isn't really much of my business, but the damn thing intrigues me. Besides, I think there is something wrong with the way the Agency and the Bureau are handling the whole thing. First of all, this is a very extraordinary situation, and they are using fairly ordinary means. Second, they're tripping over each other, both hot to make the pinch, as they say. Then there's the one thing I can't really express. Something about this whole affair bothers me. It should never have happened. Both the idea behind the event and the way in which the event manifested itself are so . . . wrong, so out of place. I think it's beyond the parameters of the Agency. Not that they're incompetent—though I think they have missed one or two small points—but they're just now viewing it from the right place. Do you understand, my boy?''

Powell nodded. ''And you are in the right place, right?''

The old man smiled. ''Well, let's just say one foot is in the door. Now here's what I want you to do. Did you notice our boy's medical record? Don't bother looking, I'll tell you. He has many times the number of colds and respiratory problems he should. He often needs medical attention. Now, if you remember the transcript of the second panic call, he sneezed and said he had a cold. I'm playing a long shot that his cold is much worse, and that wherever he is, he'll come out to get help. What do you think?''

Powell shrugged. ''Might be worth a try.''

The old man was gleeful. ''I think so, too. Neither the Agency nor the Bureau has tumbled to this yet, so we have a clear field. Now, I've arranged for you to head a special team of D.C. detectives—never mind how I managed it, I did. Start with the general practitioners in the metropolitan area. Find out if any of them have treated anyone like our boy—use his new description. If they haven't, tell them to report to us if they do. Make up some plausible story so they'll open up to you. One other thing. Don't let the others find out we're looking too. The last time they had a chance, two men got shot.''

Powell stood to go. ''I'll do what I can, sir.''

''Fine, fine, my boy. I knew I could count on you. I'm

still thinking on this. If I come up with anything else, I'll let you know. Good luck.''

Powell left the room. When the door was shut, the old man smiled.

While Kevin Powell began his painstakingly dull check of the Washington medical community, a very striking man with strange eyes climbed out of a taxi in front of Sunny's Surplus. The man had spent the morning reading a Xeroxed file identical with the one Powell had just examined. He had received the file from a very distinguished-looking gentleman. The man with the strange eyes had a plan for finding Malcolm. He spent an hour driving around the neighborhood, and now he began to walk it. At bars, newspaper stands, public offices, private buildings, anywhere a man could stop for a few minutes, he would stop and show an artist's projected sketch of Malcolm with short hair. When people seemed reluctant to talk to him, the man flashed one of five sets of credentials the distinguished man had obtained. By 3:30 that afternoon he was tired, but it didn't show. He was more resolute than ever. He stopped at a Hot Shoppe for coffee. On the way out he flashed the picture and a badge at the cashier in a by now automatic manner. Almost anyone else would have registered the shock he felt when the clerk said she recognized the man.

"Yeah, I saw the son of a bitch. He threw his money at me he was in such a hurry to leave. Ripped a nylon crawling after a rolling nickel.''

"Was he alone?''

"Yeah, who would want to be with a creep like that?''

"Did you see which way he went?''

"Sure I saw. If I'd have had a gun I'd have shot him. He went that way.''

The man carefully paid his bill, leaving a dollar tip for the cashier. He walked in the direction she had pointed. Nothing, no reason to make a man looking for safety hurry that particular way. Then again . . . He turned into the parking lot and became a D.C. detective for the fat man in the felt hat.

"Sure, I seen him. He got into the car with the chick."

The striking man's eyes narrowed. "What chick?"

"The one that works for them lawyers. The firm rents space for all the people that work there. She ain't so great to look at, but she's got class, if you know what I mean."

"I think so," said the fake detective, "I think so. Who is she?"

"Just a minute." The man in the hat waddled into a small shack. He returned carrying a ledger. "Let's see, lot 63 . . . lot 63. Yeah, here it is. Ross, Wendy Ross. This here is her Alexandria address."

The narrow eyes glanced briefly at the offered book and recorded what they saw. They turned back to the man in the felt hat. "Thanks." The striking man began to walk away.

"Don't mention it. Say, what's this guy done?"

The man stopped and turned back. "Nothing, really. We're just looking for him. He . . . he's been exposed to something—it couldn't hurt you—and we just want to make sure he's all right."

Ten minutes later the striking man was in a phone booth. Across the city a distinguished-looking gentleman picked up a private phone that seldom rang. "Yes," he said, then recognized the voice.

"I have a firm lead."

"I knew you would. Have someone check it out, but don't let him act on it unless absolutely unavoidable circumstances arise. I want you to handle it personally so there will be no more mistakes. Right now I have a more pressing matter for your expert attention."

"Our sick mutual friend?"

"Yes. I'm afraid he has to take a turn for the worse. Meet me at place four as soon as you can." The line went dead.

The man stayed in the phone booth long enough to make another short call. Then he hailed a taxi and rode away into the fading light.

A small car parked across and up the street from Wendy's apartment just as she brought a tray of stew to Malcolm. The driver could see Wendy's door very clearly, even though he had to bend his tall, thin body into a very strange position. He watched the apartment, waiting.

"Overconfidence breeds error when we take for granted that the game will continue on its normal course; when we fail to provide for an unusually powerful resource—a check, a sacrifice, a stalemate. Afterwards the victim may wail, 'But who could have dreamt of such an idiotic-looking move?'"

—Fred Reinfeld, *The Complete Chess Course*

Saturday

"Are you feeling any better?"

Malcolm looked up at Wendy and had to admit that he

was. The pain in his throat had subsided to a dull ache and almost twenty-four hours of sleep had restored a good deal of his strength. His nose still ran most of the time and talking brought pain, but even these discomforts were slowly fading.

As the discomforts of his body decreased, the discomforts of his mind increased. He knew it was Saturday, two days after his co-workers had been killed and he had shot a man. By now several very resourceful, very determined groups of people would be turning Washington upside down. At least one group wanted him dead. The others probably had little affection for him. In a dresser across the room lay $9,382 stolen from a dead man, or at least removed from his apartment. Here he was, lying sick in bed without the foggiest notion about what had happened or what he was to do. On top of all that, here on his bed sat a funny-looking girl wearing a T shirt and a smile.

"You know, I really don't understand it," he rasped. He didn't. In all the hours he had devoted to the problem he could find only four tentative assumptions that held water: that the Agency had been penetrated by somebody; that somebody had hit his section; that somebody had tried to frame Heidegger as a double by leaving the "hidden" money; and that somebody wanted him dead.

"Do you know what you're going to do yet?" Wendy used her forefinger to trace the outline of Malcolm's thigh under the sheet.

"No." He said exasperatedly, "I might try the panic number later tonight, if you'll take me to a phone booth."

She leaned forward and lightly kissed his forehead. "I'll take you anywhere." She smiled and lightly kissed him, his eyes, his cheek, down to his mouth, down to his neck.

Flipping back the sheet, she kissed his chest, down to his stomach, down.

Afterwards they showered and he put in his contacts. He went back to bed. When Wendy came back into his room, she was fully dressed. She tossed him four paperbacks. "I didn't know what you liked, but these should keep you busy while I'm gone."

"Where are—" Malcolm had to pause and swallow. It still hurt. "Where are you going?"

She smiled. "Silly boy, I've got to shop. We're low on food and there are still some things you need. If you're very good—and you're not bad—I might bring you a surprise." She walked away but turned back at the door. "If the phone rings, don't answer unless it rings twice, stops, then rings again. That'll be me. Aren't I learning how to be a good spy? I'm not expecting anybody. If you're quiet, no one will know you're here." Her voice took on a more serious tone. "Now, don't worry, OK? You're perfectly safe here." She turned and left.

Malcolm had just picked up one book when her head popped around the doorjamb. "Hey," she said, "I just thought of something. If I get strep throat, will it classify as venereal disease?" Malcolm missed when he threw the book at her.

When Wendy opened her door and walked to her car, she didn't notice the man in the van parked across the street stirring out of lethargy. He was a plain-looking man. He wore a bulky raincoat even though spring sunshine ruled the morning. It was almost as if he knew the good weather couldn't last. The man watched Wendy pull out of the parking lot and drive away. He looked at his watch. He would wait three minutes.

* * *

Saturday is a day off for most government employees, but not for all. This particular Saturday saw a large number of civil servants from various government levels busily and glumly drawing overtime. One of these was Kevin Powell. He and his men had talked to 216 doctors, receiving nurses, interns, and other assorted members of the medical profession. Over half the general practitioners and throat specialists in the Washington area had been questioned. It was now eleven o'clock on a fine Saturday morning. All Powell had to report to the old man behind the mahogany desk could be summed up in one word: nothing.

The old man's spirits weren't dimmed by the news. "Well, my boy, just keep on trying, that's all I can say, just keep on trying. If it's any consolation, let me say we're in the same position as the others, only they have run out of things to do except watch. But one thing has happened: Weatherby is dead."

Powell was puzzled. "I thought you said his condition was improving."

The old man spread his hands. "It was. They planned to question him late last night or early this morning. When the interrogation team arrived shortly after one A.M., they found him dead."

"How?" Powell's voice held more than a little suspicion.

"How indeed? The guard on the door swears only medical personnel went in and out. Since he was in the Langley hospital, I'm sure security must have been tight. His doctors say that, given the shock and the loss of blood, it is entirely possible he died from the wound. They were sure he was doing marvelously. Right now they're doing a complete autopsy."

"It's very strange."

"Yes, it is, isn't it? But because it's strange, it should have been almost predictable. The whole case is strange. Ah, well, we've been over this ground before. I have something new for you."

Powell leaned closer to the desk. He was tired. The old man continued, "I told you I wasn't satisfied with the way the Agency and the Bureau were handling the case. They've run into a blind wall. I'm sure part of the reason is that their method led them there. They've been looking for Malcolm the way a hunter looks for any game. While they're skilled hunters, they're missing a thing or two. I want you to start looking for him as though you were the prey. You've read all the information we have on him, you've been to his apartment. You must have some sense of the man. Put yourself in his shoes and see where you end up.

"I have a few helpful tidbits for you. We know he needed transportation to get wherever he is. If nothing else, a man on foot is visible, and our boy wants to avoid that. The Bureau is fairly certain he didn't take a cab. I see no reason to fault their investigation along those lines. I don't think he would ride a bus, not with the package the man at the store sold him. Besides, one never knows who one might meet on a bus.

"So there's your problem. Take a man or two, men who can put themselves in the right frame of mind. Start from where he was last seen. Then, my boy, get yourself hidden the way he has."

Just before Powell opened the door, he looked at the smiling old man and said, "There's one other thing that's strange about this whole business, sir. Malcolm was never trained as a field agent. He's a researcher, yet look how well he's made out.''

"Yes, that is rather strange," answered the old man. He smiled and said, "You know, I'm getting rather keen to meet our boy Malcolm. Find him for me, Kevin, find him for me quickly.''

Malcolm needed a cup of coffee. The hot liquid would make his throat feel better and the caffeine would pep him up. He grinned slowly, being careful not to stretch tender neck muscles. With Wendy, a man needed a lot of pep. He went downstairs to the kitchen. He had just put a pot on to boil when the doorbell rang.

Malcolm froze. The gun was upstairs, right next to his bed where he could reach it in a hurry, provided, of course, that he was in bed. Quietly, Malcolm tiptoed to the door. The bell rang again. He sighed with relief when he saw through the one-way glass peephole that it was only a bored-looking mailman, his bag slung over one shoulder, a package in one hand. Then he became annoyed. If he didn't answer the door, the mailman might keep coming back until he delivered his package. Malcolm looked down at his body. He only had on jockey shorts and a T shirt. Oh well, he thought, the mailman's probably seen it all before. He opened the door.

"Good morning, sir, how are you today?''

The mailman's cheer seemed to infect Malcolm. He smiled back, and said hoarsely, "Got a little cold. What can I do for you?''

"Got a package here for a Miss . . .'' The mailman paused and slyly smiled at Malcolm. ''A Miss Wendy Ross. Special delivery, return receipt requested.''

"She's not here right now. Could you come back later?"

The mailman scratched his head. "Well, could, but it would sure be easier if you signed for it. Hell, government don't care who signs, long as it's signed."

"OK," said Malcolm. "Do you have a pen?"

The mailman slapped his pockets unsuccessfully.

"Come on in," Malcolm said. "I'll get one."

The mailman smiled as he entered the room. He closed the door behind him. "You're making my day a lot easier by going to all this trouble," he said.

Malcolm shrugged. "Think nothing of it." He turned and went into the kitchen to find a pen. As he walked through the door, his mind abstractedly noted that the mailman had put the package down and was unslinging his pouch.

The mailman was very happy. His orders had been to determine whether Malcolm was in the apartment, to reconnoiter the building, and to make a hit only if it could be done with absolute safety and certainty. He knew a bonus would follow his successful display of initiative in hitting Malcolm. The girl would come later. He pulled the silenced sten gun out of his pouch.

Just before Malcolm came around the corner from the kitchen he heard the click when the mailman armed the sten gun. Malcolm hadn't found a pen. In one hand he carried the coffeepot and in the other an empty cup. He thought the nice mailman might like some refreshment. That Malcolm didn't die then may be credited to the fact that when he turned the corner and saw the gun swinging toward him he didn't stop to think. He threw the pot of boiling coffee and the empty cup straight at the mailman.

The mailman hadn't heard Malcolm coming. His first thought centered on the objects flying toward his face. He threw up his arms, covering his head with the gun. The coffeepot bounced off the gun, but the lid flew off and hot coffee splashed down on bare arms and an upturned face.

Screaming, the mailman threw the gun away from him. It skidded across the floor, stopping under the table holding Wendy's stereo. Malcolm made a desperate dive for it, only to be tripped by a black loafer. He fell to his hands and staggered up. He quickly looked over his shoulder and ducked. The mailman flew over Malcolm's head. Had the flying side kick connected, the back of Malcolm's head would have shattered and in all probability his neck would have snapped.

Even though he hadn't practiced in a dojo for six months, the mailman executed the difficult landing perfectly. However, he landed on the scatter rug Wendy's grandmother had given her as a birthday present. The rug slid along the waxed floor and the mailman fell to his hands. He bounced up twice as fast as Malcolm.

The two men stared at each other. Malcolm had at least ten feet to travel before he could reach the gun on his right. He could probably beat the mailman to the table, but before he could pull the gun out the man would be all over his back. Malcolm was closest to the door, but it was closed. He knew he wouldn't have the precious seconds it would take to open it.

The mailman looked at Malcolm and smiled. With the toe of his shoe he tested the hardwood floor. Slick. With deft, practiced movements he slipped his feet out of the loafers. He wore slipperlike socks. These too came off when he rubbed his feet on the floor. The mailman came prepared to walk quietly, barefoot, and his preparations served him in an unexpected manner. His bare feet hugged the floor.

Malcolm looked at his smiling opponent and began to accept death. He had no way of knowing the man's brown belt proficiency, but he knew he didn't stand a chance. Malcolm's knowledge of martial arts was almost negligible. He had read fight scenes in numerous books and seen them in movies. He had had two fights as a child, won one, lost one. His physical education instructor in college had spent three hours teaching the class some cute tricks he had learned in the Marines. Reason made Malcolm try to copy the man's stance, legs bent, fists clenched, left arm in front and bent perpendicular to the floor, right arm held close to the waist.

Very slowly the mailman began to shuffle across the fifteen feet that separated him from his prey. Malcolm began to circle toward his right, vaguely wondering why he bothered. When the mailman was six feet from Malcolm he made his move. He yelled and with his left arm feinted a backhand snap at Malcolm's face. As the mailman anticipated, Malcolm ducked quickly to his right side. When the mailman brought his left hand back, he dropped his left shoulder and whirled to his right on the ball of his left foot. At the end of the three-quarters circle his right leg shot to meet Malcolm's ducking head.

But six months is too long to be out of practice and expect perfect results, even when fighting an untrained amateur. The kick missed Malcolm's face, but thudded into his left shoulder. The blow knocked Malcolm into the wall. When he bounced off he barely dodged the swinging hand chop follow-through blow.

The mailman was very angry with himself. He had missed twice. True, his opponent was injured, but he should have been dead. The mailman knew he must get back into practice before he met an opponent who knew what to do.

A good karate instructor will emphasize that karate is three-quarters mental. The mailman knew this, so he devoted his entire mind to the death of his opponent. He concentrated so deeply he failed to hear Wendy as she opened and shut the door, quietly so as not to disturb Malcolm's sleeping. She had forgotten her checkbook.

Wendy was dreaming. It wasn't real, these two men standing in her living room. One her Malcolm, his left arm twitching to life at his side. The other a short, stocky stranger standing so strangely, his back toward her. Then she heard the stranger very softly say, "You've caused enough trouble!" and she knew it was all frighteningly real. As the stranger began to shuffle toward Malcolm, she carefully reached around the kitchen corner, and took a long carving knife from a sparkling set held on the wall by a magnet. She walked toward the stranger.

The mailman heard the click of heels on the hardwood floor. He quickly feinted toward Malcolm and whirled to face the new challenge. When he saw the frightened girl standing with a knife clutched awkwardly in her right hand, the worry that had been building in his brain ceased. He quickly shuffled toward her, dodging and dipping as she backed away trembling. He let her back up until she was about to run into the couch, then he made his move. His left foot snapped forward in a roundhouse kick and the knife flew from her numbed hand. His left knuckles split the skin just beneath her left cheekbone in a vicious backhand strike. Wendy sank, stunned, to the couch.

But the mailman had forgotten an important maxim of multiple-attackers situations. A man being attacked by two or more opponents must keep moving, delivering quick, alternate attacks to each of his opponents. If he stops to concentrate on one before all of his opponents have been neutralized, he leaves himself exposed. The mailman should have whirled to attack Malcolm immediately after the kick. Instead he went for the *coup de grâce* on Wendy.

By the time the mailman had delivered his backhand blow to Wendy, Malcolm had the sten gun in his hand. He could use his left arm only to prop the barrel up, but he lined the gun up just as the mailman raised his left hand for the final downward chop.

"Don't!"

The mailman whirled toward his other opponent just as Malcolm pulled the trigger. The coughing sounds hadn't stopped before the mailman's chest blossomed with a red, spurting row. The body flew over the couch and thudded on the floor.

Malcolm picked Wendy up. Her left eye began to puff shut and a trickle of blood ran down her cheek. She sobbed quietly, "My God, my God, my God."

It took Malcolm five minutes to calm her down. He peered cautiously through the blinds. No one was in sight. The yellow van across the street looked empty. He left Wendy downstairs with the machine gun huddled in her arms pointed at the door. He told her to shoot anything that came through. He quickly dressed, and packed his money, his clothes, and the items Wendy had bought him in one of her spare suitcases. When he came downstairs, she was more rational. He sent her upstairs to pack. While she was gone, he searched the corpse and found nothing. When she came down ten minutes later, her face had been washed and she carried a suitcase.

Malcolm took a deep breath and opened the door. He had a coat draped over his revolver. He couldn't bring himself to take the sten gun. He knew what it had done. No one shot him. He walked to the car. Still no bullets. No one was even visible. He nodded to Wendy. She ran to the car dragging their bags. They got in and he quietly drove away.

Powell was tired. He and two other Washington detectives were covering covered ground, walking along all the streets in the area where Malcolm had last been sighted. They questioned people at every building. All they found were people who had been questioned before. Powell was leaning against a light pole, trying to find a new idea, when he saw one of his men hurrying toward him.

The man was Detective Andrew Walsh, Homicide. He grabbed Powell's arm to steady himself. "I think I've found something, sir." Walsh paused to catch his breath. "You know how we've found a lot of people who were questioned before? Well, I found one, a parking-lot attendant, who told the cop who questioned him something that isn't in the official reports."

"For Christ's sake, *what?*" Powell was no longer tired.

"He made Malcolm, off a picture this cop showed him. More than that, he told him he saw Malcolm get into a car with this girl. Here's the girl's name and address."

"When did all this happen?" Powell began to feel cold and uneasy.

"Yesterday afternoon."

"Come on!" Powell ran down the street to the car, a panting policeman in his wake.

They had driven three blocks when the phone on the dash buzzed. Powell answered. "Yes?"

"Sir, the medical survey team reports a Dr. Robert Knudsen identified Condor's picture as the man he treated for strep throat yesterday. He treated the suspect at the apartment of a Wendy Ross, R-o . . ."

Powell cut the dispatcher short. "We're on our way to her apartment now. I want all units to converge on the area, but do not approach the house until I get there. Tell them to get there as quickly but as quietly as they can. Now give me the chief."

A full minute passed before Powell heard the light vice come over the phone. "Yes, Kevin, what do you have?"

"We're on our way to Malcolm's hideout. Both groups hit on it at about the same time. I'll give you details alter. There's one other thing: somebody with official credentials has been looking for Malcolm and not reporting what he finds."

There was a long pause, then the old man said, "This could explain many things, my boy. Many things. Be very careful. I hope you're in time." The line went dead. Powell hung up, and resigned himself to the conclusion that he was probably much too late.

Ten minutes later Powell and three detectives rang Wendy's doorbell. They waited a minute, then the biggest man kicked the door in. Five minutes later Powell summed up what he found to the old man.

"The stranger is unidentifiable from here. His postman's uniform is a fake. The silenced sten gun was probably used during the hit on the Society. The way I see it, he and someone else, probably our boy Malcolm, were fighting. Malcolm beat him to the gun. I'm sure it's the mailman's because his pouch is rigged to carry it. Our boy's luck seems to be holding very well. We've found a picture of the girl, and we've got her car license number. How do you want to handle it?''

"Have the police put out an APB on her for . . . murder. That'll throw our friend who's monitoring us and using our credentials. Right now, I want to know who the dead man is, and I want to know fast. Send his photo and prints to every agency with a priority rush order. Do not include any other information. Start your teams looking for Malcolm and the girl. Then I guess we have to wait.''

A dark sedan drove by the apartment as Powell and the others walked toward their cars. The driver was tall and painfully thin. His passenger, a man with striking eyes hidden behind sunglasses, waved him on. No one noticed them drive past.

Malcolm drove around Alexandria until he found a small, dumpy used-car lot. He parked two blocks away and sent Wendy to make the purchase. Ten minutes later, after having sworn she was Mrs. A. Edgerton for the purpose of registration and paid an extra hundred dollars cash, she drove off in a slightly used Dodge. Malcolm followed her to a park. They transferred the luggage and removed the license plates from the Corvair. Then they loaded the Dodge and slowly drove away.

Malcolm drove for five hours. Wendy never spoke during the whole trip. When they stopped at the Parisburg, Virginia, motel, Malcolm registered as Mr. and Mrs. Evans. He parked the car behind the motel "so it won't get dirty from the traffic passing by." The old lady running the motel merely shrugged and went back to her TV. She had seen it before.

Wendy lay very still on the bed. Malcolm slowly undressed. He took his medicine and removed his contacts before he sat down next to her.

"Why don't you undress and get some sleep, honey?"

She turned and looked at him slowly. "It's real, isn't it." Her voice was softly matter-of-fact. "The whole thing is real. And you killed that man. In my apartment, you killed a man."

"It was either him or us. You know that. You tried, too."

She turned away. "I know." She got up and slowly undressed. She turned off the light and climbed into bed. Unlike before, she didn't snuggle close. When Malcolm went to sleep an hour later, he was sure she was still awake.

"Where there is much light there is also much shadow."

—Goethe

SUNDAY

"Ah, Kevin, we seem to be making progress."

The old man's crisp, bright words did little to ease the numbness gripping Powell's mind. His body ached, but the discomfort was minimal. He had been conditioned for much more severe strains than one missed rest period. But during three months of rest and recuperation, Powell had become accustomed to sleeping late on Sunday mornings. Additionally, the frustration of his present assignment irritated him. So far his involvement had been *post facto*. His two years of training and ten years' experience were being used to run errands and gather information. Any cop could do that, and many cops were. Powell didn't share the old man's optimism.

"How, sir?" Frustrated as he was, Powell spoke respectfully. "Some trace of Condor and the girl?"

"No, not yet." Despite a very long night, the old man sparkled. "There's still a chance she bought that car, but it hasn't been seen. No, our progress is from another angle. We've identified the dead man."

Powell's mind cleared. The old man continued.

"Our friend was once Calvin Lloyd, sergeant, United States Marine Corps. In 1959 he left that group rather suddenly while stationed in Korea as an adviser to a South Korean Marine unit. There is a good chance he was mixed up in the murder of a Seoul madam and one of her girls. The Navy could never find any direct evidence, but they think the madam and he were running a base commuter service and had a falling-out over rebates. Shortly after the bodies were found, Lloyd went AWOL. The Marines didn't look for him very hard. In 1961 Navy Intelligence received a report indicating he had died rather suddenly in Tokyo. Then in 1963 he was identified as one of several arms dealers in Laos. Evidently his job was technical advice. At the time, he was linked to a man called Vincent Dale Maronick. More on Maronick later. Lloyd dropped out of sight in 1965, and until yesterday he was again believed dead."

The old man paused. Powell cleared his throat, signaling that he wanted to speak. After receiving a courteous nod, Powell said, "Well, at least we know that much. Besides telling us a small who, how does it help?"

The old man held up his left forefinger. "Be patient, my boy, be patient. Let's take our steps slowly and see what paths cross where.

"The autopsy on Weatherby yielded only a probability, but based on what has happened, I'm inclined to rate it very high. There is a chance his death may be due to an air bubble in the blood, but the pathologists won't swear to it. His doctors insist the cause must be external—and therefore not their fault. I'm inclined to agree with them. It's a pity for us Weatherby isn't around for questioning, but for someone it's a very lucky break. Far too lucky, if you ask me.

"I'm convinced Weatherby was a double agent, though for whom I have no idea. The files that keep turning up missing, our friend with credentials covering the town just ahead of us, the setup of the hit on the Society. They all smell of inside information. With Weatherby eliminated, it follows he could have been the leak that became too dangerous for someone. Then there's that whole shooting scene behind the theaters. We've been over that before, but something new occurred to me.

"I had both Sparrow IV's and Weatherby's bodies examined by our Ballistics man. Whoever shot Weatherby almost amputated his leg with the bullet. According to our man it was at least a .357 magnum with soft lead slugs. But Sparrow IV had only a neat round hole in his throat. Our Ballistics man doesn't think they were shot with the same gun. That, plus the fact Weatherby wasn't killed, makes the whole thing look fishy. I think our boy Malcolm, for some reason or other, shot Weatherby and then ran. Weatherby was hurt, but not hurt so bad he couldn't eliminate witness Sparrow IV. But that's not the interesting piece of news.

"From 1958 until late 1969, Weatherby was stationed in

Asia, primarily out of Hong Kong, but with stints in Korea, Japan, Taiwan, Laos, Thailand, Cambodia, and Vietnam. He worked his way up the structure from special field agent to station head. You'll note he was there during the same period as our dead mailman. Now for a slight but very interesting digression. What do you know about the man called Maronick?''

Powell furrowed his brow. "I think he was some sort of special agent. A freelancer, as I recall."

The old man smiled, pleased. "Very good, though I'm not sure if I understand what you mean by 'special.' If you mean extremely competent, thorough, careful, and highly successful, then you're correct. If you mean dedicated and loyal to one side, then you are very wrong. Vincent Maronick was—or is, if I'm not mistaken—the best freelance agent in years, maybe the best of this century for his specialty. For a short-term operation requiring cunning, ruthlessness, and a good deal of caution, he was the best money could buy. The man was tremendously skilled. We're not sure where he received his training, though it's clear he was American. His individual abilities were not so outstanding that they couldn't be matched. There were and are better planners, better shots, better pilots, better saboteurs, better everything in particular. But the man had a persevering drive, a toughness that pushed his capabilities far beyond those of his competitors. He's a very dangerous man, one of the men I could fear.

"In the early sixties he surfaced working for the French, mainly in Algeria, but, please note, also taking care of some of their remaining interests in Southeast Asia. Starting in 1963, he came to the attention of those in our business. At various times he worked for Britain, Communist China,

Italy, South Africa, the Congo, Canada, and he even did two stints for the Agency. He also did a type of consulting service for the IRA and the OAS (against his former French employers). He always gave satisfaction, and there were no reports of any failures. He was very expensive. Rumor has it he was looking for a big score. Exactly why he was in the business isn't clear, but my guess is it was the one field that allowed him to use his talents to the fullest and reap rewards quasi-legally. Now here's the interesting part.

"In 1964 Maronick was employed by the Generalissimo on Taiwan. Ostensibly he was used for actions against mainland China, but at the time the General was having trouble with the native Taiwanese and some dissidents among his own immigrant group. Maronick was employed to help preserve order. Washington wasn't pleased with some of the Nationalist government's internal policies. They were afraid the General's methods might be a little too heavy-handed for our good. The General refused to agree, and began to go his own merry way. At the same time, we began to worry about Maronick. He was just too good and too available. He had never been employed against us, but it was just a matter of time. The Agency decided to terminate Maronick, as both a preventive measure and as a subtle hint to the General. Now, who do you suppose was station agent out of Taiwan when the Maronick termination order came through?"

Powell was 90 percent sure, so he ventured, "Weatherby?"

"Right you are. Weatherby was in charge of the termination operation. He reported it successful, but with a hitch. The method was a bomb in Maronick's billet. Both the Chinese agent who planted the bomb and Maronick were killed. Naturally, the explosion obliterated both bodies. Weatherby verified the hit as an eyewitness.

"Now let's back up a little. Whom do you suppose Maronick employed as an aide on at least five different missions?"

It wasn't a guess. Powell said, "Our dead mailman, Sergeant Calvin Lloyd."

"Right again. Now here's yet another clincher. We never had much on Maronick, but we did have a few foggy pictures, sketchy descriptions, whatnot. Guess whose file is missing?" The old man didn't even give Powell a chance to speak before he answered his own question. "Maronick's. Also, we have no records of Sergeant Lloyd. Neat, yes?"

"Yes indeed." Powell was still puzzled. "What makes you think Maronick is involved?"

The old man smiled. "Just playing an inductive hunch. I racked my brain for a man who could and would pull a hit like the one on the Society. When, out of a dozen men, Maronick's file turned up missing, my curiosity rose. Navy Intelligence sent over the identification of Lloyd, and his file noted he had worked with Maronick. Wheels began to turn. When they both linked up with Weatherby, lights flashed and a band played. I spent a very productive morning making my poor old brain work when I should have been feeding pigeons and smelling cherry blossoms."

The room was silent while the old man rested and Powell thought. Powell said, "So you figure Maronick is running some kind of action against us and Weatherby was doubling for him, probably for some time."

"No," said the old man softly, "I don't think so."

The old man's reply surprised Powell. He could only stare and wait for the soft voice to continue.

"The first and most obvious question is why. Given all that has happened and the way in which it has happened, I don't think the question can practically and logically be approached. If it can't be approached logically, then we are starting from an erroneous assumption, the assumption that the CIA is the central object of an action. Then there's the next question of who. Who would pay—and I imagine pay dearly—for Maronick with Weatherby's duplicity and at least Lloyd's help to have us hit in the way we have been hit? Even given that phony Czech revenge note, I can think of no one. That, of course, brings us back to the why question, and we're spinning our wheels in a circle going nowhere. No, I think the proper and necessary question to ask and answer is not who or why, but what. What is going on? If we can answer that, then the other questions and their answers will flow. Right now, there is only one key to that what, our boy Malcolm."

Powell sighed wearily. "So we're back to where we started from, looking for our lost Condor."

"Not exactly where we started from. I have some of my men digging rather extensively in Asia, looking for whatever it is that ties Weatherby, Maronick, and Lloyd together. They may find nothing, but no one can tell. We also have a better idea of the opposition, and I have some men looking for Maronick."

"With all the machinery you have at your disposal we should be able to flush one of the two, Malcolm or Maronick—sounds like a vaudeville team, doesn't it?"

"We're not using the machinery, Kevin. We're using us, plus what we can scrounge from the D.C. police."

Powell choked. "What the hell! You control maybe fifty men, and the cops can't give you much. The Agency has hundreds of people working on this thing now, not counting the Bureau and the NSA and the others. If you give them what you have given me, they could . . ."

Quietly but firmly the old man interrupted. "Kevin, think a moment. Weatherby was the double in the Agency, possibly with some lower-echelon footmen. He, we assume, acquired the false credentials, passed along the needed information, and even went into the field himself. But if he was the double, then who arranged for his execution, who knew the closely guarded secret of where he was and enough about the security setup to get the executioner (probably the competent Maronick) in and out again?" He paused for the flicker of understanding on Powell's face. "That's right, another double. If my hunch is correct, a very highly placed double. We can't risk any more leaks. Since we can't trust anyone, we'll have to do it ourselves."

Powell frowned and hesitated before he spoke. "May I make a suggestion, sir?"

The old man deliberately registered surprise. "Why, of course you may, my dear boy! You are supposed to use your fine mind, even if you are afraid of offending your superior."

Powell smiled slightly. "We know, or at least we are assuming, there is a leak, a fairly highly placed leak. Why don't we keep after Malcolm but concentrate on stopping the leak from the top? We can figure out what group of people the leak could be in and work on them. Our surveillance should catch them even if so far they haven't left a trail. The pressure of this thing will force them to do something. At the very least, they must keep in touch with Maronick."

"Kevin," the old man replied quietly, "your logic is sound, but the conditions for your assumptions invalidate your plan. You assume we can identify the group of people who could be the source of the leak. One of the troubles with our intelligence community—indeed, one of the reasons for my own section—is that things are so big and so complicated such a group easily numbers over fifty, probably numbers over a hundred, and may run as high as two hundred persons. That's if the leak is conscious on their part. Our leak may be sloppy around his secretary, or his communications man may be a double.

"Even if the leak is not of a secondary nature, through a secretary or a technician, such surveillance would be massive, though not impossible. You've already pointed out my logistical limitations. In order to carry out your suggestion, we would need the permission and assistance of some of the people in the suspect group. That would never do.

"We also have a problem inherent in the group of people with whom we would be dealing. They are professionals in the intelligence business. Don't you think they might tumble to our surveillance? And even if *they* didn't, each one of their departments has its own security system we would have to avoid. For example, officers in Air Force Intelligence are subject to unscheduled spot checks, including surveillance and phone taps. It's done both to see if the officers are honest and to see if someone else is watching them. We would have to avoid security teams *and* a wary, experienced suspect.

"What we have," the old man said, placing the tips of his fingers together, "is a classic intelligence problem. We have possibly the world's largest security and intelligence organization, an entity ironically dedicated to both stopping the flow of information from and increasing the flow to this country. At a moment's notice we can assign a hundred trained men to dissect a fact as minuscule as a misplaced luggage sticker. We can turn the same horde loose on any given small group and within a few days we would know everything the group did. We can bring tremendous pressure to bear on any point we can find. There lies the problem: on this case we can't find the point. We know there's a leak in our machine, but until we can isolate the area it's in, we can't dissect the machine to try to pinpoint the leak. Such activity would be almost certainly futile, and possibly dangerous, to say nothing of awkward. Besides, the moment we start looking, the opposition will know we know there's a leak.

"The key to this whole problem is Malcolm. He might be able to pinpoint the leak for us, or at least steer us in a particular direction. If he does, or if we turn up any links between Maronick's operation and someone in the intelligence community, we will, of course, latch on to the suspect. But until we have a firm link, such an operation would be sloppy, hit-and-miss work. I don't like that kind of job. It's inefficient and usually not productive."

Powell covered his embarrassment with a formal tone. "Sorry, sir. I guess I wasn't thinking."

The old man shook his head. "On the contrary, my boy," he exclaimed, "you were thinking, and that's very good. It's the one thing we've never been able to train our people to do, and it's one thing these massive organizations tend to discourage. It's far better to have you thinking and proposing schemes which, shall we say, are hastily considered and poorly conceived, here in the office, than it is for you to be a robot in the street reacting blindly. That gets everyone into trouble, and it's a good way to wind up dead. Keep thinking, Kevin, but be a little more thorough."

"So the plan is still to find Malcolm and bring him home safe, right?"

The old man smiled. "Not exactly. I've done a lot of thinking about our boy Malcolm. He is our key. They, whoever they are, want our boy dead, and want him dead badly. If we can keep him alive, *and* if we can make him troublesome enough to them so that they center their activities on his demise, then we have turned Condor into a key. Maronick and company, by concentrating on Malcolm, make themselves into their own lock. If we are careful and just a shade lucky, we can use the key to open the lock. Oh, we still have to find our Condor, and quickly, before anyone else does. I'm making some additional arrangements to aid us along that line too. But when we find him, we prime him.

"After you've had some rest, my assistant will bring you instructions and any further information we receive."

As Powell got up to go, he said, "Can you give me anything on Maronick?"

The old man said, "I'm having a friend in the French secret service send over a copy of their file on the flight from Paris. It won't arrive until tomorrow. I could have had it quicker, but I didn't want to alert the opposition. Outside of what you already know, I can only tell you that physically Maronick is reportedly a very striking man."

Malcolm began to wake just as Powell left the old man's office. For a few seconds he lay still, remembering all that had happened. Then a soft voice whispered in his ear, "Are you awake?"

Malcolm rolled over. Wendy rested on one elbow, shyly

looking at him. His throat felt better and he sounded almost normal when he said, "Good morning."

Wendy blushed. "I'm . . . I'm sorry about yesterday, I mean how mean I was. I just . . . I just have never seen or done anything like that and the shock . . ."

Malcolm shut her up with a kiss. "It's OK. It was pretty horrible."

"What are we going to do now?" she asked.

"I don't know for sure. I think we should hole up here for at least a day or two." He looked around the sparsely furnished room. "It may be a little dull."

Wendy looked up at him and grinned. "Well, not too dull." She kissed him lightly, then again. She pulled his mouth down to her small breast.

Half an hour later they still hadn't decided anything.

"We can't do that *all* the time," Malcolm said at last.

Wendy made a sour face and said, "Why not?" But she sighed acceptance. "I know what we can do!" She leaned half out of the bed and groped on the floor. Malcolm grabbed her arm to keep her from falling.

"What the hell are you doing?" he said.

"I'm looking for my purse. I brought some books we can read out loud. You said you liked Yeats." She rummaged under the bed. "Malcolm, I can't find them, they aren't here. Everything else is in my purse, but the books are missing. I must have . . . Owww!" Wendy jerked back on the bed and pried herself loose from Malcolm's suddenly tightened grip. "Malcolm, what are you doing? That hurt . . ."

"The books. The missing books." Malcolm turned and looked at her. "There is something about those missing books that's important! That has to be the reason!"

Wendy was puzzled. "But they're only poetry books.

You can get them almost anywhere. I probably just forgot to bring them.''

"Not those books, the Society's books, the ones Heidegger found missing!'' He told her the story.

Malcolm felt the excitement growing. "If I can tell them about the missing books, it'll give them something to start on. The reason my section was hit must have been the books. They found out Heidegger was digging up old records. They had to hit everybody in case someone else knew. If I can give the Agency those pieces, maybe they can put the puzzle together. At least I'll have something more to give them than my story about how people get shot wherever I go. They frown on that.''

"But how will you tell the Agency? Remember what happened the last time you called them?''

Malcolm frowned. "Yes, I see what you mean. But the last time they set up a meeting. Even if the opposition has penetrated the Agency, even if they know what goes over the Panic Line, I still think we're OK. With all that has gone on, I imagine dozens of people must be involved. At least some of them will be clean. They'll pass on what I phone in. It should ring some right bells somewhere.'' He paused for a moment. "Come on, we have to go back to Washington.''

"Hey, wait a minute!'' Wendy's outstretched hand missed its grasp on Malcolm's arm as he bounded out of bed and into the bathroom. "Why are we going back there?''

The shower turned on. "Have to. A long-distance phone call can be traced in seconds, a local one takes longer.'' The tempo of falling water on metal walls increased.

"But we might get killed!''

"What?''

Wendy yelled, but she tried to be as quiet as possible. "I said we might be killed."

"Might get killed here too. You scrub my back and I'll scrub yours."

"I'm very disappointed, Maronick." The sharp words cut through the strained air between the two men. The distinguished-looking speaker knew he had made a mistake when he saw the look in his companion's eyes.

"My name is Levine. You will remember that. I suggest you do not make a slip like that again." The striking man's crisp words undercut the other man's confidence, but the distinguished-looking gentleman tried to hide his discomposure.

"My slip is minor compared to the others that have been happening," he said.

The man who wished to be called Levine showed no emotion to the average eye. An acute observer who had known him for some time *might* have detected the slight flush of frustrated anger and embarrassment.

"The operation is not yet over. There have been setbacks, but there has been no failure. Had there been failure, neither of us would be here." As if to emphasize his point, he gestured toward the crowds milling around them. Sunday is a busy day for tourists at the Capitol building.

The distinguished-looking man regained his confidence. In a firm whisper he said, "Nevertheless there have been setbacks. As you so astutely pointed out, the operation is not yet over. I need not remind you that it was scheduled for completion three days ago. Three days. A good deal can happen in three days. For all our bumbling we have been very lucky. The longer the operation continues, the greater the risk that certain things will come to the fore. We both know how disastrous that could be."

"Everything possible is being done. We must wait for another chance."

"And if we don't get another chance? What then, my fine friend, what then?"

The man called Levine turned and looked at him. Once again the other man felt nervous. Levine said, "Then we make our chance."

"Well, I certainly hope there will be no more...setbacks."

"I anticipate none."

"Good. I shall keep you informed of all the developments in the Agency. I expect you to do the same with me. I think there is nothing further to say."

"There is one other thing," Levine said calmly. "Operations such as this sometimes suffer certain kinds of internal setbacks. Usually these...setbacks happen to certain personnel. These setbacks are planned by operation directors, such as yourself, and they are meant to be permanent. The common term for such a setback is double cross. If I were my director, I would be most careful to avoid any such setback, don't you agree?" The pallor crossing the other man's face told Levine there was no disagreement. Levine smiled politely, nodded farewell, and walked away. The distinguished man watched him stalk down the marble corridors and out of sight. The gentleman shuddered slightly, then went home to Sunday brunch with his wife, son, and a fidgety new daughter-in-law.

While Malcolm and Wendy dressed and the two men left the Capitol grounds, a telephone truck pulled up to the outer gates at Langley. After the occupants and their mission were cleared, they proceeded to the communications center. The two telephone repairmen were accompanied by a special security officer on loan from another branch. Most of the Agency men were looking for a man called Condor. The security officer had papers identifying him as Major David Burros. His real name was Kevin Powell, and the two telephone repairmen, ostensibly there to check the telephone tracing device, were highly trained Air Force electronics experts flown in from Colorado less than four hours before. After their mission was completed, they would be quarantined for three weeks. In addition to checking the tracing device, they installed some new equipment and made some complicated adjustments in the wiring of the old. Both men tried to keep calm while they worked from wiring diagrams labeled Top Secret. Fifteen minutes after they began work, they electronically signaled a third man in a phone booth four miles away. He called a number, let it ring until he received another signal, then hung up and walked quickly away. One of the experts nodded at Powell. The three men gathered their tools and left as unobtrusively as they had come.

An hour later Powell sat in a small room in downtown Washington. Two plainclothes policemen sat outside the door. Three of his fellow agents lounged in chairs scattered around the room. There were two chairs at the desk where Powell sat, but one was unoccupied. Powell talked into one of the two telephones on the desk.

"We're hooked up and ready to go, sir. We've tested the device twice. It checked out from our end and our man in the Panic Room said everything was clear there. From now on, all calls made to Condor's panic number will ring here. If it's our boy, we'll have him. If it's not . . . Well, let's hope we can fake it. Of course, we can also nullify the bypass and just listen in.''

The old man's voice told his delight. ''Excellent, my boy, excellent. How's everything else working out?''

''Marian says the arrangements with the *Post* should be complete within the hour. I hope you realize how much our ass is in the fire on this. Someday we'll have to tell the Agency we tapped their Panic Line, and they won't appreciate that at all.''

The old man chuckled. ''Don't worry about that, Kevin. It's been in the fire before and it will be there again. Besides, theirs is roasting too, and I imagine they won't feel too bad if we pull it out for them. Any reports from the field?''

''Negative. Nobody reports a sign of Malcolm or the girl. When our boy goes to ground, he goes to ground.''

''Yes, I was thinking much the same thing myself. I don't think the opposition has got him. I'm rather proud of his efforts so far. Do you have my itinerary?''

''Yes, sir. We'll call you if anything happens.'' The old man hung up, and Powell settled down for what he hoped would be a short wait.

Wendy and Malcolm arrived in Washington just as the sun was setting. Malcolm drove to the center of the city. He parked the car at the Lincoln Memorial, removed their luggage, and locked the vehicle securely. They came into Washington via Bethesda, Maryland. In Bethesda they purchased some toiletries, clothes, a blond wig, and a large padded ''visual disguise and diversionary'' bra for Wendy, a roll of electrical tape, some tools, and a box of .357 magnum shells.

Malcolm took a carefully calculated risk. Using Poe's ''Purloined Letter'' principle that the most obvious hiding place is often the safest, he and Wendy boarded a bus for Capitol Hill. They rented a tourist room on East Capitol Street less than a quarter of a mile from the Society. The proprietress of the dingy hostel welcomed the Ohio honeymooners. Most of her customers had checked out and headed home after a weekend of sightseeing. She didn't even care if they had no rings and the girl had a black eye. In order to create a believable image of loving young marrieds (or so Malcolm whispered), the young couple retired early.

"In war it is not men, but the man who counts."

—*Napoleon*

Monday, Morning to Midafternoon

The shrill scream from the red phone jarred Powell from his fitful nap. He grabbed the receiver before a second ring. The other agents in the room began to trace and record the call. Concentrating on listening, Powell only half saw their scurrying figures in the morning light. He took a deep breath and said, "493–7282."

The muffled voice on the other end seemed far away. "This is Condor."

Powell began the carefully prepared dialogue. "I read

you, Condor. Listen closely. The Agency has been penetrated. We're not sure who, but we're pretty sure it's not you." Powell cut the beginning of a protest short. "Don't waste time protesting your innocence. We accept it as a working assumption. Now, why did you shoot Weatherby when they came to pick you up?"

The voice on the other end was incredulous. "Didn't Sparrow IV tell you? That man—Weatherby?—shot at me! He was parked outside the Society Thursday morning. In the same car."

"Sparrow IV is dead, shot in the alley."

"I didn't . . ."

"We know. We think Weatherby did. We know about you and the girl." Powell paused to let this sink in. "We traced you to her apartment and found the corpse. Did you hit him?"

"Barely. He almost got us."

"Are you injured?"

"No, just a little stiff and woozy."

"Are you safe?"

"For the time being, fairly."

Powell leaned forward tensely and asked the hopeless and all-important question. "Do you have any idea why your group was hit?"

"Yes." Powell's sweaty hand tightened on the receiver as Malcolm quickly told of the missing books and financial discrepancies Heidegger had discovered.

When Malcolm paused, Powell asked in a puzzled voice, "But you have no idea what it all means?"

"None. Now, what are you going to do about getting us to safety?"

Powell took the plunge. "Well, that's going to be a little

problem. Not just because we don't want you set up and hit, but because you're not talking to the Agency.''

Five miles away, in a phone booth at a Holiday Inn, Malcolm's stomach began to churn. Before he could say anything, Powell spoke again.

''I can't go into the details. You will simply have to trust us. Because of the penetration of the Agency at what is probably a very high level, we've taken over. We plugged into the Panic Line and intercepted your call. Please don't hang up. We've got to blow the double in the Agency and find out what this was all about. You're our only way, and we want you to help us. You have no choice.''

''Bullshit, man! You might be another security agency, and then again you might not. Even if you are OK, why the hell should I help you? This isn't my kind of work! I read about this stuff, not do it.''

''Consider the alternatives.'' Powell's voice was cold. ''Your luck can't hold forever, and some very determined and competent people besides us are looking for you. As you said, this isn't your line of work. Someone will find you. Without us, all you can do is hope that the right someone does find you. If we're the right someone, then everything is already OK. If we're not, then at least you know what we want you to do. It's better than running blind. Any time you don't like our instructions, don't follow them. There's one final clincher. We control your communication link with the Agency. We even have a man on the listed line.'' (This was a lie.) ''The only other way you can go home is to show up at Langley in person. Do you like the idea of going in there cold?''

Powell paused and got no answer. ''I thought not. It won't be too dangerous. All we basically want is for you to stay hidden and keep rattling the opposition's cage. Now, here's what we know so far." Powell gave Malcolm a concise rundown of all the information he had. Just as he finished, his man in charge of tracing the call came to him and shrugged his shoulders. Puzzled, Powell continued. "Now, there's another way we can communicate with you. Do you know how to work a book code?"

"Well . . . You better go over it again."

"OK. First of all pick up a paperback copy of *The Feminine Mystique*. There is only one edition. Got that? OK. Now, whenever we want to communicate with you, we will run an ad in the *Post*. It will appear in the first section, and the heading will read, 'Today's Lucky Sweepstakes Winning Numbers Are:' followed by a series of hyphenated numbers. The first number of each series is the page number, the second is the line number, and the third is the word number. When we can't find a corresponding word in the book, we'll use a simple number-alphabet code. A is number one, B is number two, and so on. When we code such a word, the first number will be thirteen. The *Post* will forward any communication you want to send us if you address it to yourself, care of Lucky Sweepstakes, Box 1, *Washington Post*. Got it?"

"Fine. Can we still use the Panic Line?"

"We'd rather not. It's very chancy."

Powell could see the trace man across the room whispering furiously into another phone. Powell said, "Do you need anything?"

"No. Now, what is it you want me to do?"

"Can you call the Agency back on your phone?"

"For a conversation as long as this?"

"Definitely not. It should only take a minute or so."

"I can, but I'll want to shift to another phone. Not for at least half an hour."

"OK. Call back and we will let the call go through. Now, here's what we want you to say." Powell told him the plan. When both men were satisfied, Powell said, "One more thing. Pick a neighborhood you won't have to be in."

Malcolm thought for a moment. "Chevy Chase."

"OK," Kevin said. "You will be reported in the Chevy Chase area in exactly one hour. Thirty minutes later a Chevy Chase cop will be wounded while chasing a man and a woman answering your descriptions. That should make everyone concentrate their forces in Chevy Chase, giving you room to move. Is that enough time?"

"Make it an hour later, OK?"

"OK."

"One more thing. Who am I talking to, I mean personally?"

"Call me Rogers, Malcolm." The connection went dead. No sooner had Powell placed the phone in the cradle than his trace man ran to him.

"Do you know what that little son of a bitch did? Do you know what he did?" Powell could only shake his head. "I'll tell you what he did, that little son of a bitch. He drove all over town and wired pay phones together, then called and hooked them all up so they transmitted one call through the lines, but each phone routed the call back through the terminal. We traced the first one in a little over a minute. Our surveillance team got there right away. They found an empty phone booth with homemade Out of Order signs and his wiring job. They had to call back for a trace on the other phone. We've gone through three traces already and there are probably more hookups to go, that son of a bitch!"

Powell leaned back and laughed for the first time in days.

When he found the part in Malcolm's dossier that mentioned his summer employment with the telephone company, he laughed again.

Malcolm left the phone booth and walked to the parking lot. In a rented U-Haul pickup with Florida plates a chesty blond wearing sunglasses sat chewing gum. Malcolm stood in the shade for a few moments while he checked the lot. Then he walked over and climbed in the truck. He gave Wendy the thumbs-up sign, then began to chuckle.

"Hey," she said, "what is it? What's so funny?"

"You are, you dummy."

"Well, the wig and the falsies were your idea! I can't help it if . . ." His protesting hand cut her short.

"That's only part of it," he said, still laughing. "If you could only see yourself."

"Well, I can't help it if I'm good." She slumped in the seat. "What did they say?"

As they drove to another phone booth, Malcolm told her.

Mitchell had been manning the Panic phone since the first call. His cot lay a few feet from his desk. He hadn't seen the sun since Thursday. He hadn't showered. When he went to the bathroom the phone followed. The head of the Panic Section was debating whether to give him pep shots. The Deputy Director had decided to keep Mitchell on the phone, as he stood a better chance than a new man of recognizing Malcolm should he call again. Mitchell was tired, but he was still a tough man. Right now he was a tough *determined* man. He was raising his ten-o'clock coffee to his lips when the phone rang. He spilled the coffee as he grabbed the receiver.

"493–7282."

"This is Condor."

"Where the hell . . ."

"Shut up. I know you're tracing this call, so there isn't much time. I would stay on your line, but the Agency has been penetrated."

"What!"

"Somebody out there is a double. The man in the alley"—Malcolm almost slipped and said "Weatherby" —"shot at me first. I recognized him from when he was parked in front of the Society Thursday morning. The other man in the alley must have told you that, though, so . . ." Malcolm slowed, anticipating interruption. He got it.

"Sparrow IV was shot. You . . ."

"I didn't do it! Why would I want to do it? Then you didn't know?"

"All we know is we have two more dead people than when you first called."

"I might have killed the man who shot at me, but I didn't kill Maronick."

"Who?"

"Maronick, the man called Sparrow IV."

"That wasn't Sparrow IV's name."

"It wasn't? The man I shot yelled for Maronick after he hit the ground. I figured Maronick was Sparrow IV." (Easy, thought Malcolm, don't overdo it.) "Never mind that now, time is running short. Whoever hit us was after something Heidegger knew. He told all of us about something strange he found in the records. He said he was going to tell somebody out at Langley. That's why I figure there is a double. Heidegger told the wrong man.

"Listen, I've stumbled onto something. I think I might be

able to figure some more out. I found something at Heidegger's place. I think I can work it out if you give me time. I know you must be looking for me. I'm afraid to come in or let you find me. Can you pull the heat off me until I figure out what I know that makes the opposition want me dead?''

Mitchell paused for a moment. The trace man frantically signaled him to keep Malcolm talking. "I don't know if we can or not. Maybe if . . .''

"There's no more time. I'll call you back when I find out some more.'' The line went dead. Mitchell looked at his trace man and got a negative shake of the head.

"How the hell do you figure that?''

Mitchell looked at the speaker, a security guard. The man in the wheelchair shook his head. "I don't, but it's not my job to figure it. Not this one.'' Mitchell looked around the room. His glance stopped when it came to a man he recognized as a veteran agent. "Jason, does the name Maronick mean anything to you?''

The nondescript man called Jason slowly nodded his head. "It rings a bell.''

"Me too,'' said Mitchell. He picked up a phone. "Records? I want everything you got on people called Maronick, any spelling you can think of. We'll probably want several copies before the day is out, so hop to it.'' He broke the connection, then dialed the number of the Deputy Director.

While Mitchell waited to be connected with the Deputy Director, Powell connected with the old man. "Our boy did fine, sir.''

"I'm delighted to hear that, Kevin, delighted.''

In a lighter voice Powell said, "Just enough truth mingled with some teasing tidbits. It'll start the Agency rolling the right way, but hopefully they won't catch up to us. If you're right, our friend Maronick may begin to feel nervous. They'll be more anxious than ever to find our Condor. Anything new on your end?''

"Nothing. Our people are still digging into the past of all concerned. Outside of us, only the police know about the connection between Malcolm and the man killed in the girl's apartment. The police are officially listing it and her disappearance as parts of a normal murder case. When the time is right, that little tidbit will fall into appropriate hands. As far as I can tell, everything is going exactly according to plan. Now I suppose I'll have to go to another dreary meeting with a straight face, gently prodding our friends in the right direction. I think it best if you stay on the line, monitoring, not intercepting, but be ready to move any time.''

"Right, sir.'' Powell hung up. He looked at the grinning men in the room and settled back to enjoy a cup of coffee.

"I'll be damned if I can make head or tail of it!'' The Navy captain thumped his hand on the table to emphasize his point, then leaned back in his spacious padded chair. The room was stuffy. Sweat stains grew under the Captain's armpits. Of all the times for the air conditioning to break down, he thought.

The Deputy Director said patiently, "None of us are really too sure what it means, either, Captain.'' He cleared his throat to take up where he had been cut off. "As I was saying, except for the information we received from Condor—however accurate it may be—we are really no further than at our last meeting.''

The Captain leaned to his right and embarrassed the man

from the FBI sitting next to him by whispering, "Then why call the God damn meeting?" The withering glance from the Deputy Director had no effect on the Captain.

The Deputy continued. "As you know, Maronick's file is missing. We've requested copies of England's files. An Air Force jet should have them here in three hours. I would like any comments you gentlemen might have."

The man from the FBI spoke immediately. "I think Condor is partially right. The CIA has been penetrated." His colleague from the Agency squirmed. "However, I think we should put it in the past tense and say 'had' been penetrated. Obviously Weatherby was the double. He probably used the Society as some sort of courier system and Heidegger stumbled onto it. When Weatherby found out, the Society had to be hit. Condor was a loose end that had to be tied up. Weatherby goofed. There are probably some members of his cell still running around, but I think fate has sealed the leak. As I see it, the important thing for us to do now is bring in Condor. With the information he can give us, we can try to pick up those few remaining men—including this Maronick, if he exists—and find out how much information we've lost."

The Deputy Director looked around the room. Just as he was about to close the meeting, the old man caught his eye.

"Might I make an observation or two, Deputy?"

"Of course, sir. Your comments are always welcome."

The men in the room shifted slightly to pay better attention. The Captain shifted too, though obviously out of frustrated politeness.

Before he spoke, the old man looked curiously at the representative from the FBI. "I must say I disagree with our colleague from the Bureau. His explanation is very plausible, but there are one or two discrepancies I find disturbing. If Weatherby was the top agent, then how and why did he die? I know it's a debatable question, at least until the lab men finish those exhaustive tests they've been making. I'm sure they will find he was killed. That kind of order would have to come down from a high source. Besides, I feel there is something wrong with the whole double agent–courier explanation. Nothing for sure, just a hunch. I think we should continue pretty much as we have been, with two slight changes.

"One, pry into the background of all concerned and look for crossing paths. Who knows what we may find? Two, let's give the Condor a chance to fly. He may find something yet. Loosen up the hunt for him, and concentrate on the background search. I have some other ideas I would like to work on for your next meeting, if you don't mind. That's all I have now. Thank you, Deputy."

"Thank you, sir. Of course, gentlemen, the ultimate decision lies with the director of the Agency. However, I've been assured our recommendations will carry weight. Until we have a definite decision, I plan to continue as we have been."

The old man looked at the Deputy Director and said, "You may be sure we shall give you whatever assistance we can."

Immediately the FBI man snapped, "That goes for us too!" He glared at the old man and received a curious smile in reply.

"Gentlemen," said the Deputy Director, "I would like to thank all of you for the assistance you have given us, now as well as in the past. Thank you all for coming. You'll be notified of the next meeting. Good day."

As the men were leaving, the FBI man glanced at the old man. He found himself staring into a pair of bright, curious eyes. He quickly left the room. On the way out, the Navy captain turned to mutter to a representative from the Treasury Department, "Jesus, I wish I had stayed on line duty! These dull meetings wear me out." He snorted, put on his naval cap, and strode from the room. The Deputy was the last to leave.

"I don't like this at all."

The two men strolled along the Capitol grounds just on the edges of the shifting crowds. The afternoon tourist rush was waning, and some government workers were leaving work early. Monday is a slow day for Congress.

"I don't like it, either, my fine friend, but we have to contend with the situation as it is, not as we wish it." The older man surveyed his striking companion and continued, "However, we at least know a little more than before. For example, we know now how important it is that Condor dies."

"I think he shouldn't be the only one." The rare Washington wind carried the striking man's voice to his companion, who shivered in spite of the warm weather.

"What do you mean?"

The reply was tinged with disgust. "It doesn't make sense. Weatherby was a tough, experienced agent. Even though he was shot, he managed to kill Sparrow IV. Do you really believe a man like that would yell out my name? Even if he made a slip, why would he yell for me? It doesn't make sense."

"Pray tell, then, what does make sense?"

"I can't say for sure. But there's something we don't know going on. Or at least something I don't know."

Nervous shock trembled in the distinguished man's voice. "Surely you're not suggesting I'm withholding information from you?"

The wind filled the long pause. Slowly, Levine-Maronick answered. "I don't know. I doubt it, but the possibility exists. Don't bother to protest. I'm not moving on the possibility. But I want you to remember our last conversation."

The men walked in silence for several minutes. They left the Capitol grounds and began to stroll leisurely past the Supreme Court building on East Capitol Street. Finally the older man broke the silence. "Do your men have anything new?"

"Nothing. We've been monitoring all the police calls and communications between the Agency and Bureau teams. With only three of us, we can't do much field work. My plan is to intercept the group that picks Condor up before they get him to a safe house. Can you arrange for him to be brought to a certain one, or at least find out what advance plans they've made? It will cut down on the odds quite a bit." The older man nodded, and Maronick continued.

"Another thing that strikes me wrong is Lloyd. The police haven't linked him with this thing yet, as far as I can tell. Condor's prints must have been all over that place, yet the police either haven't lifted them—which I doubt—or reported them on the APB. I don't like that at all. It doesn't fit. Could you check on that in such a way that you don't stir them into activity?"

The older man nodded again. The two men continued their stroll, apparently headed home from work. By now they were three blocks from the Capitol, well into the residential area. Two blocks down the street a city bus pulled over to the side, belched diesel smoke, and deposited a small group of commuters on the sidewalk. As the bus pulled away, two of the commuters detached themselves from the group and headed toward the Capitol.

Malcolm had debated about turning in the rented pickup. It gave them relatively private transportation, but it was conspicuous. Pickups are not common in Washington, especially pickups emblazoned with "Alfonso's U-Haul, Miami Beach." The truck also ran up a bill, and Malcolm wanted to keep as much of his money in reserve as he could. He decided public transportation would suffice for the few movements he planned. Wendy halfheartedly agreed. She liked driving the pickup.

It happened when they were almost abreast of the two men walking toward them on the other side of the street. The gust of wind proved too strong for the bobby pin holding Wendy's loose wig. It jerked the blond mass of hair from her head, throwing it into the street. The wig skidded to a stop and lay in an ignoble heap almost in the center of the road.

Excited and shocked, Wendy cried out, "Malcolm, my wig! Get it, get it!" Her shrill voice carried above the wind and the slight traffic. Across the street Levine-Maronick pulled his companion to an abrupt halt.

Malcolm knew Wendy had made a mistake by calling out his name. He silenced her with a gesture as he stepped between the parked cars and into the street on a retrieval mission. He noticed the two men across the street watching him, so he tried to appear nonchalant, perhaps embarrassed for his wife.

Levine-Maronick moved slowly but deliberately, his keen

eyes straining at the couple across the street, his mind making point-by-point comparisons. He was experienced enough to ignore the shock of fantastic coincidence and concentrate on the moment. His left hand unbuttoned his suit coat. Out of the corner of his eye and in the back of his mind Malcolm saw and registered all this, but his attention centered on the lump of hair at his feet. Wendy reached him just as he straightened up with the wig in his hands.

"Oh, shit, the damned thing is probably ruined." Wendy grabbed the tangled mass from Malcolm. "I'm glad we don't have far to go. Next time I'll use two . . ."

Maronick's companion had been out of the field too long. He stood on the sidewalk, staring at the couple across the street. His intent gaze attracted Malcolm's attention just as the man incredulously mouthed a word. Malcolm wasn't sure of what the man said, but he knew something was wrong. He shifted his attention to the man's companion, who had emerged from behind a parked car and begun to cross the street. Malcolm noticed the unbuttoned coat, the waiting hand flat against the stomach.

"Run!" He pushed Wendy away from him and dove over the parked sports car. As he hit the sidewalk, he hoped he was making a fool of himself.

Maronick knew better than to run across an open area charging a probably armed man hiding behind bulletproof cover. He wanted to flush his quarry for a clear shot. He also knew part of his quarry was escaping. That had to be prevented. When his arm stopped moving, his body had snapped into the classic shooting stance, rigid, balanced. The stubby revolver in his right hand barked once.

Wendy had taken four very quick steps when it occurred to her she didn't know why she was running. This is silly, she thought, but she slowed only slightly. She dodged between two parked cars and slowed to a jog. Four feet from the shelter of a row of tour buses she turned her head, looking over her left shoulder for Malcolm.

The steel-jacketed bullet caught her at the base of the skull. It spun her up and around, slowly, like a marionette ballerina turning on one tiny foot.

Malcolm knew what the shot meant, but he still had to look. He forced his head to the left and saw the strange, crumpled form on the sidewalk twenty feet away. She was dead. He knew she was dead. He had seen too many dead people in the last few days to miss that look. A stream of blood trickled downhill toward him. The wig was still clutched in her hand.

Malcolm had his gun out. He raised his head and Maronick's revolver cracked again. The bullet screeched across the car's hood. Malcolm ducked. Maronick quickly began to angle across the street. He had four rounds left, and he allowed two of them for further harassing fire.

Capitol Hill in Washington has two ironic qualities: it has both one of the highest crime rates and one of the highest concentrations of policemen in the city. Maronick's shots and the screams of frightened tourists brought one of the traffic policemen on the run. He was a short, portly man named Arthur Stebbins. In five more years he planned to retire. He lurched toward the scene of a possible crime with full confidence that a score of fellow officers were only seconds behind him. The first thing he saw was a man edging across the street, a gun in his hand. This was also the last thing he saw, for Maronick's bullet caught him square in the chest.

Maronick knew he was in trouble. He had hoped for

another minute before the police arrived. By that time Condor would have been dead, and he could be far away. Now he saw two more blue forms a block away. They were tugging at their belts. Maronick swiftly calculated the odds, then turned, looking for a way out.

At this instant a rather bored congressional aide heading home from the Rayburn House Office Building drove up the side street just behind Maronick. The aide stopped his red Volkswagen beetle to check for traffic on the main artery. Like many motorists, he paid little attention to the areas he passed through. He barely realized what happened when Maronick jerked his door open, pulled him from the car, whipped the pistol across his face, and then sped away in the beetle.

Maronick's companion stood still through the whole episode. When he saw Maronick make his getaway, he too took flight. He ran up East Capitol Street. Less than fifty feet from the scene he climbed into his black Mercedes Benz and sped away. Malcolm raised his head in time to see the license plate of the car.

Malcolm looked down the street to the policemen. They huddled around the body of their comrade. One of them spoke into his belt radio, calling in the description of Maronick and the red Volkswagen and asking for reinforcements and an ambulance. It dawned on Malcolm that they hadn't seen him yet, or that if they had, they thought of him as only a passerby-witness to a police killing. He looked around him. The people huddled behind parked cars and along the clipped grass were too frightened to yell until he was out of sight. He quickly walked away in the direction the Volkswagen had come. Just before he turned the corner he looked back at the crumpled form on the sidewalk. A policeman was bending over Wendy's still body. Malcolm swallowed and turned away. Three blocks later he caught a cab and headed downtown. As he sat in the back seat, his body shook slightly, but his mind burned.

"The first step toward becoming a skilful defensive player, then, is to handle the defense in an aggressive spirit. If you do that, you can find subtle defensive resources that other players would not dream of. By seeking active counterplay, you will often upset clever attacking lines. Better yet, you will upset your opponent."

—Fred Reinfeld, The Complete Chess Course

Late Monday

"All hell has broken loose, sir." Powell's voice reflected the futility he felt.

"What do you mean?" On the other end of the telephone line the old man strained to catch every word.

"The girl has been shot on Capitol Hill. Two witnesses tentatively identified that old photo of Maronick. They also identified the girl's companion who fled as Malcolm. As far as we can tell, Malcolm wasn't injured. Maronick got a cop, too."

"Killing two people in one day makes Maronick rather busy."

"I didn't say she was dead, sir."

After an almost imperceptible pause the tight voice said, "Maronick is not known for missing. She is dead, isn't she?"

"No, sir, although Maronick didn't miss by much. Another fraction of an inch and he would have splattered her brain all over the sidewalk. As it is, she has a fairly serious head wound. She's in the Agency hospital now. They had to do a little surgery. This time I made the security arrangements. We don't want another Weatherby. She's unconscious. The doctors say that she'll probably stay that way for a few days, but they think she'll eventually be OK."

The old man's voice had an eager edge as he asked, "Was she able to tell anyone anything, anything at all?"

"No, sir," Powell replied disappointedly. "She's been unconscious since she was shot. I've got two of my men in her room. Besides double-checking everyone who comes in, they're waiting in case she wakes up.

"We've got another problem. The police are mad. They want to go after Maronick with everything they've got. A dead cop and a wounded girl on Capitol Hill mean more to them than our spy chase. I've been able to hold them back, but I don't think I can for long. If they start looking using the tie-ins they know, the Agency is bound to find out. What should I do?"

After a pause, the old man said, "Let them. Give them a slightly sanitized report of everything we know, enough to give them some leads on Maronick. Tell them to go after him with everything they can muster, and tell them they'll have lots of help. The only thing we must insist on is first questioning rights once they get him. Insist on that, and tell them I can get authority to back up our claim. Tell them to find Malcolm too. Does it look like Maronick was waiting for them?"

"Not really. We found the boardinghouse used by Malcolm

and the girl. I think Maronick was in the neighborhood and just happened to spot them. If it hadn't been for the police, he probably would have nailed Condor. There's one other thing. One witness swears Maronick wasn't alone. He didn't get a good look at the other man, but he says the guy was older than Maronick. The older man disappeared.''

''Any confirmation from other witnesses?''

''None, but I tend to believe him. The other man is probably the main double we are after. The Hill is an excellent rendezvous. That could explain Maronick stumbling onto Malcolm and the girl.''

''Yes. Well, send me everything you can on Maronick's friend. Can the witness make an ID sketch or a license-plate number? Anything?''

''No, nothing definite. Maybe we'll get lucky and the girl can help us with that if she wakes up soon.''

''Yes,'' the old man said softly, ''that would be lucky.''

''Do you have any instructions?''

The old man was silent for a few moments, then said, ''Put an ad—no, better make it two ads—in the *Post*. Our boy, wherever he is, will expect to hear from us. But he's probably not too organized, so put a simple, uncoded ad to run on the same page as the coded one. Tell him to get in touch with us. In the coded ad tell him the girl is alive, the original plan is off, and we're trying to find some way to bring him in safe. We'll have to take the chance that he either has or can get a copy of the code book. We can't say anything important in the uncoded ad because we don't know who else besides our boy might be reading the *Post*.''

''Our colleagues will guess something is up when they see the uncoded ad.''

''That's an unpleasant fact, but we knew we would have

to face them eventually. However, I think I can manage them."

"What do you think Malcolm will do?"

There was another short pause before the old man replied. "I'm not sure," he said. "A lot depends on what he knows. I'm sure he thinks the girl is dead. He would have responded differently to the situation if he thought she was alive. We may be able to use her somehow, as bait for either Malcolm or the opposition. But we'll have to wait and see on that."

"Anything else you want me to do?"

"A good deal, but nothing I can give you instructions for. Keep looking for Malcolm, Maronick, and company, anything which might explain this mess. And keep in touch with me, Kevin. After the meeting with our colleagues, I'll be at my son's house for dinner."

"I think it's disgusting!" The man from the FBI leaned across the table to glare at the old man. "You knew all along that the murder in Alexandria was connected with this case, yet you didn't tell us. What's worse, you kept the police from reporting it and handling it according to form. Disgusting! Why, by now we could have traced Malcolm and the girl down. They would both be safe. We would be hot after the others, provided, of course, that we didn't already have them. I've heard of petty pride, but this is national security! I can assure you, we at the Bureau would not behave in such a manner!"

The old man smiled. He had told them only about the link between Maronick and the murder in Alexandria. Imagine their anger if they realized how much more he knew! He glanced at the puzzled faces. Time to mend fences, or at least to rationalize. "Gentlemen, gentlemen, I can understand your anger. But of course you realize I had a reason for my actions.

"As you all know, I believe there is a leak in the Agency. A substantial leak, I might add. It was and is my opinion that this leak would thwart our efforts on this matter. After all, the end goal—whether we admit it or not—is to plug that very leak. Now, how was I to know that the leak was not in this very group? We are not immune from such dangers." He paused. The men around the table were too experienced to glance at each other, but the old man could feel the tension rising. He congratulated himself.

"Now then," he continued, "perhaps I was wrong to conceal so much from the group, but I think not. Not that I'm accusing anyone—or, by the way, that I have abandoned the possibility of the leak's being here. I still think my move prudent. I also believe it wouldn't have made much difference, despite what our friend from the FBI says. I think we would still be where we are today. But that is not the question, at least not now. The question is, Where do we go from here and how?"

The Deputy Director looked around the room. No one seemed eager to respond to the old man's question. Of course, such a situation meant he should pick up the ball. The Deputy dreaded such moments. One always had to be so careful about stepping on toes and offending people. The Deputy felt far more at ease on his field missions when he only had to worry about the enemy. He cleared his throat and used a ploy he hoped the old man expected. "What are your suggestions, sir?"

The old man smiled. Good old Darnsworth. He played the game fairly well, but not very well. In a way he hated to do this to him. He looked away from his old friend and stared into space. "Quite frankly, Deputy, I'm at a loss for suggestions. I really couldn't say. Of course, I think we should keep on trying to do something.''

Inwardly the Deputy winced. He had the ball again. He looked around the table at a group of men now suddenly not so competent and eager-looking. They looked everywhere but at him, yet he knew they were watching his every move. The Deputy cleared his throat again. He resolved to end the agony as quickly as possible. ''As I see it, then, no one has any new ideas. Consequently, I have decided that we will continue to operate in the manner we have been.'' (Whatever that means, he thought.) ''If there is nothing further...'' He paused only momentarily. ''...I suggest we adjourn.'' The Deputy shuffled his papers, stuffed them into his briefcase, and quickly left the room.

As the others rose to leave, the Army Intelligence representative leaned over to the Navy captain and said, ''I feel like the nearsighted virgin on his honeymoon who couldn't get hard: I can't see what to do and I can't do it either.''

The Navy captain looked at his counterpart and said, ''I never have that problem.''

Malcolm changed taxis three times before he finally headed for northeast Washington. He left the cab on the fringes of the downtown area and walked around the neighborhood. During his ride around town he formed a plan, rough and vague, but a plan. His first step was to find all-important shelter from the hunters.

It took only twenty minutes. He saw her spot him and discreetly move in a path parallel to his. She crossed the street at the corner. As she stepped up to the sidewalk she ''tripped'' and fell against him, her body pressed close to his. Her arms ran quickly up and down his sides. He felt her body tense when her hands passed over the gun in his belt. She jerked away and a pair of extraordinarily bright brown eyes darted over his face.

"Cop?" From her voice she couldn't have been more than eighteen. Malcolm looked down at her stringy dyed blond hair and pale skin. She smelled from the perfume sampler at the corner drugstore.

"No." Malcolm looked at the frightened face. "Let's say I'm involved in a high-risk business." He could see the fear on her face, and he knew she would take a chance.

She leaned against him again, pushing her hips and her chest forward. "What are you doing around here?"

Malcolm smiled. "I want a lay. I'm willing to pay for it. Now, if I'm a cop, the bust is no good, 'cause I entrapped you. OK?"

She smiled. "Sure, tiger. I understand. What kind of party are we going to have?"

Malcolm looked down at her. Italian, he thought, or maybe Central European. "What do you charge?"

The girl looked at him, judging possibilities. It had been a slow day. "Twenty dollars for a straight lay?" She made it clear she was asking, not demanding.

Malcolm knew he had to get off the streets soon. He looked at the girl. "I'm in no hurry," he said. "I'll give you . . . seventy-five for the whole night. I'll throw in breakfast if we can use your place."

The girl tensed. It might take her a whole day and half the night to make that kind of money. She decided to gamble. Slowly she moved her hand into Malcolm's crotch, covering her action by leaning into him, pushing her breast against his arm. "Hey, honey, that sounds great, but . . ." She almost lost her nerve. "Could you make it a hundred? Please? I'll be extra-special good to you."

Malcolm looked down and nodded. "A hundred dollars. For the full night at your place." He reached in his pocket and handed her a fifty-dollar bill. "Half now, half afterwards. And don't think about any kind of setup."

The girl snatched the money from his hand. "No setup. Just me. And I'll be real good—real good. My place isn't far." She linked her arm in his to guide him down the street.

When they reached the next corner, she whispered, "Just a second, honey, I have to talk to that man." She released his arm before he could think and hurried to the blind pencil hawker on the corner. Malcolm backed against the wall. His hand shot inside his coat. The gun butt was sweaty.

Malcolm saw the girl slip the man the fifty dollars. He mumbled a few words. She walked quickly to a nearby phone booth, almost oblivious of a boy who jostled her and grinned as her breasts bounced. The sign said Out of Order, but she opened the door anyway. She looked through the book, or so Malcolm thought. He couldn't see too well, as her back was toward him. She shut the door and quickly returned.

"Sorry to keep you waiting, honey. Just a little business deal. You don't mind, do you?"

When they came abreast of the blind man, Malcolm stopped and pushed the girl away. He snatched the thick sunglasses off the man's face. Carefully watching the astonished girl, he looked at the pencil seller. The two empty sockets made him push the glasses back quicker than he had taken them off. He stuffed a ten-dollar bill into the man's cup. "Forget it, old man."

The hoarse voice laughed. "It's done forgotten, mister."

As they walked away, the girl looked at him. "What did you do that for?"

Malcolm looked down at the puzzled, dull face. "Just checking."

Her place turned out to be one room with a kitchen-bath area. As soon as they were safely inside, she bolted and locked the door. Malcolm fastened the chain. "Be right with you, honey. Take off your clothes. I'll fix you up real good right away." She darted in the curtained-off bathroom area.

Malcolm looked out the window. Three stories up. No one could climb in. Fine. The door was solid and double-locked. He didn't think anyone had followed them, or even really noticed them. He slowly took off his clothes. He put the gun on the small table next to the bed and covered it with an old *Reader's Digest*. The bed squeaked when he lay down. Both his mind and his body ached, but he knew he had to act as normal as possible.

The curtains parted and she came to him, her eyes shining. She wore a long-sleeved black nightgown. The front hung open. Her breasts dangled—long, skinny pencils. The rest of her body matched her breasts, skinny, almost emaciated. Her voice was distant. "Sorry I took so long, sugar. Let's get down to business."

She climbed on the bed and pulled his head to her breasts. "There, baby, there you go." For a few minutes she ran her hands over him, then she said, "Now I'll take real good care of you." She moved to the base of the bed and buried her head in his crotch. Minutes later she coaxed his body into a response. She got up and went to the bathroom. She returned holding a jar of Vaseline. "Oh, baby, you were real good, real good, sugar." She lay down on the bed to apply the lubricant to herself. "There, sugar, all ready for you. All ready for you whenever you want."

For a long time they lay there. Malcolm finally looked at her. Her body moved slowly, carefully, almost laboriously. She was asleep. He went to the bathroom. On the back of the stained toilet he found the spoon, rubber hose, matches, and homemade syringe. The small plastic bag was still three-quarters full of the white powder. Now he knew why the nightgown had long sleeves.

Malcolm searched the apartment. He found four changes of underwear, three blouses, two skirts, two dresses, a pair of jeans, and a red sweater to match the purple one lying on the floor. A torn raincoat hung in the closet. In a shoe box in the kitchen he found six of the possession return receipts issued upon release from a Washington jail. He also found a two-year-old high-school identification card. Mary Ruth Rosen. Her synagogue address was neatly typed on the back. There was nothing to eat except five Hersheys, some coconut, and a little grapefruit juice. He ate everything. Under the bed he found an empty Mogen David 20/20 wine bottle. He propped it against the door. If his theory worked, it would crash loudly should the door open. He picked up her inert form. She barely stirred. He put her on the torn armchair and threw a blanket over the limp bundle. It wouldn't make any difference if her body wasn't comfortable in the night. Malcolm took out his lenses and lay down on the bed. He was asleep in five minutes.

"In almost every game of chess there comes a crisis that must be recognized. In one way or another a player risks something— if he knows what he's doing, we call it a 'calculated risk.'

"If you understand the nature of this crisis; if you perceive how you've committed yourself to a certain line of play; if you can foresee you've committed yourself to a certain line of play; if you can foresee the nature of your coming task and its accompanying difficulties, all's well. But if this awareness is absent, then the game will be lost for you, and fighting back will do no good."

—*Fred Reinfeld, The Complete Chess Course*

Tuesday, Morning through Early Evening

Malcolm woke shortly after seven. He lay quietly until just before eight, his mind going over all the possibilities. In the end he still decided to carry it through. He glanced at the chair. The girl had slid onto the floor during the night. The blanket was wrapped over her head and she was breathing hard.

Malcolm got up. With a good deal of clumsy effort he put her on the bed. She didn't stir through the whole process.

The bathroom had a leaky hose and nozzle hooked up to the tub, so Malcolm took a tepid shower. He successfully shaved with the slightly used safety razor. He desperately wanted to brush his teeth, but he couldn't bring himself to use the girl's toothbrush.

Malcolm looked at the sleeping form before he left the apartment. Their agreement had been for a hundred dollars, and he had only paid her fifty. He knew where that money went. Reluctantly, he laid the other fifty dollars on the dresser. It wasn't his money anyway.

Three blocks away he found a Hot Shoppe where he breakfasted in the boisterous company of neighbors on their way to work. After he left the restaurant he went to a drugstore. In the privacy of a Gulf station rest room he brushed his teeth. It was 9:38.

He found a phone booth. With change from the Gulf station he made his calls. The first one was to Information and the second one connected him with a small office in Baltimore.

"Bureau of Motor Vehicle Registration. May I help you?"

"Yes," Malcolm replied. "My name is Winthrop Estes, of Alexandria. I was wondering if you could help me pay back a favor."

"I'm not sure what you mean."

"You see, yesterday as I was driving home from work, my battery tipped over right in the middle of the street. I got it hooked up again, but there wasn't enough charge to fire the engine. Just as I was about to give up and try to push the thing out of the way, this man in a Mercedes Benz pulled up behind me. At great risk to his own car, he gave me the push necessary to get mine started. Before I had a chance to even thank him, he drove away. All I got was his license number. Now, I would at least like to send him a thank-you note or buy him a drink or something. Neighborly things like that don't happen very often in D.C."

The man on the other end of the line was touched. "They certainly don't. With his Mercedes! Phew, that's some nice guy! Let me guess. He had Maryland plates and you want me to check and see who he is, right?"

"Right. Can you do it?"

"Well... Technically no, but for something like this, what's a little technicality? Do you have the number?"

"Maryland 6E–49387."

"6E–49387. Right. Hold on just one second and I'll have it." Malcolm heard the receiver clunk on a hard surface. In the background, footsteps faded into a low office murmur of typewriters and obscure voices, then grew stronger. "Mr. Estes? We've got it. Black Mercedes sedan, registered to a Robert T. Atwood, 42 Elwood—that's E-l-w-o-o-d—Lane, Chevy Chase. Those people must really be loaded. That's *the* country-squire suburb. He could probably afford a scratch or two on his car. Funny, those people usually don't give a damn, if you know what I mean."

"I know what you mean. Listen, thanks a lot."

"Hey, don't thank me. For something like this, glad to do it. Only don't let it get around, know what I mean? Might tell Atwood the same thing, OK?"

"OK."

"You sure you got it? Robert Atwood, 42 Elwood Lane, Chevy Chase?"

"I've got it. Thanks again." Malcolm hung up and stuffed the piece of paper with the address on it into his pocket. He wouldn't need it to remember Mr. Atwood. For no real reason, he strolled back to the Hot Shoppe for coffee. As far as his watchful eyes could tell, no one noticed him.

The morning *Post* lay on the counter. On impulse he

began to thumb through it. It was on page 12. They hadn't taken any chances. The three-inch ad was set in bold type and read, "Condor call home."

Malcolm smiled, hardly glancing at the coded sweepstakes ad. If he called in, they would tell him to come home or at least lie low. That wasn't what he intended. There was nothing they could say in the coded message that could make any difference to him. Not now. Their instructions had lost all value yesterday on Capitol Hill.

Malcolm frowned. If his plan went wrong, the whole thing might end unsatisfactorily. Undoubtedly that end would also mean Malcolm's death, but that didn't bother him too much. What bothered him was the horrible waste factor that failure would mean. He had to tell someone, somehow, just in case. But he couldn't let anyone know, not until he had tried. That meant delay. He had to find a way of delayed communication.

The sign flashing across the street gave him the inspiration. With the materials he had at hand he began to write. Twenty minutes later he stuffed curt synopses of the last five days and a prognosis for the future into three small envelops begged from the waitress. The napkins went to the FBI. The pieces of junk paper from his wallet filled the envelope addressed to the CIA. The map of D.C. he had picked up at the Gulf station went to the *Post*. These three envelopes went into a large manila envelope he bought at the drugstore. Malcolm stuck the big envelope in a mailbox. Pickup was scheduled for 2:00 P.M. The big envelope was addressed to Malcolm's bank, which for some reason closed at 2:00 P.M. on Tuesdays. Malcolm reckoned it would take the bank until at least tomorrow to find and mail the letters. He had a minimum of twenty-four hours to operate in, and he had passed on what he knew. He considered himself free of obligations.

While Malcolm spent the rest of the day standing in the perpetually long line at the Washington Monument, security and law-enforcement agencies all over the city were quietly going bananas. Detectives and agents tripped over each other and false reports of Malcolm. Three separate carloads of officials from three separate agencies arrived simultaneously at the same boarding house to check out three separate leads, all of which were false. The proprietress of the boardinghouse still had no idea what happened after the officials angrily drove away. A congressional intern who vaguely resembled Malcolm's description was picked up and detained by an FBI patrol. Thirty minutes after the intern was identified and released from federal custody, he was arrested by Washington police and again detained. Reporters harassed already nervous officials about the exciting Capitol Hill shootout. Congressmen, senators, and political hacks of every shade kept calling the agencies and each other, inquiring about the rumored security leak. Of course, everyone refused to discuss it over the phone, but the senator-congressman-department chief wanted to be personally briefed. Kevin Powell was trying once again to play Condor and retrace Malcolm. As he walked along East Capitol Street, puzzling, perturbing questions kept disturbing the lovely spring day. He received no answers from the trees and buildings, and at 11:00 he gave up the chase to meet the director of the hunt.

Powell was late, but when he walked quickly into the room he did not receive a reproachful glance from the old man. Indeed, the old man's congeniality seemed at a new height. At first Powell thought the warmth was contrived for the benefit of the stranger who sat with them at the small table, but he gradually decided it was genuine.

The stranger was one of the biggest men Powell had ever seen. It was hard to judge his height while he sat, but Powell guessed he was at least six feet seven. The man had a massive frame, with at least three hundred pounds of flesh supplying extra padding beneath the expensively tailored suit. The thick black hair was neatly greased down. Powell noticed the man's little piggy eyes quietly, carefully taking stock of him.

"Ah, Kevin," said the old man, "how good of you to join us. I don't believe you know Dr. Lofts."

Powell didn't know Dr. Lofts personally, but he knew the man's work. Dr. Crawford Lofts was probably the foremost psychological diagnostician in the world, yet his reputation was known only in very tightly controlled circles. Dr. Lofts headed the Psychiatric Evaluation Team for the Agency. PET Came into its own when its evaluation of the Soviet Premier convinced President Kennedy that he should go ahead with the Cuban blockade. Ever since then, PET had been given unlimited resources to compile its evaluation of major world leaders and selected individuals.

After ordering coffee for Powell, the old man turned and said, "Dr. Lofts has been working on our Condor. For the last few days he has talked to people, reviewed our boy's work and dossiers, even lived in his apartment. Trying to build an action profile, I believe they call it. You can explain it better, Doctor."

The softness of Loft's voice surprised Powell. "I think you've about said it, old friend. Basically, I'm trying to find out what Malcolm would do, given the background he has.

About all I can say is that he will improvise fantastically and ignore whatever you tell him unless it fits into what he wants." Dr. Lofts did not babble about his work at every opportunity. This too surprised Powell, and he was unprepared when Lofts stopped talking.

"Uh, what are you doing about it?" Powell stammered, feeling very foolish when he heard his improvised thoughts expressed out loud.

The Doctor rose to go. At least six-seven. "I've got field workers scattered at points throughout the city where Malcolm might turn up. If you'll excuse me, I want to get back to supervising them." With a curt, polite nod to the old man and Powell, Dr. Lofts lumbered from the room.

Powell looked at the old man. "Do you think he has much of a chance?"

"No, no more than anyone else. That's what he thinks, too. Too many variables for him to do much more than guess. The realization of that limitation is what makes him good."

"Then why bring him in? We can get all the manpower we want without having to pull in PET."

The old man's eyes twinkled, but there was coldness in his voice. "Because, my dear boy, it never hurts to have a lot of hunters if the hunters are hunting in different ways. I want Malcolm very badly, and I don't want to miss a trick. Now, how are you coming from your end?"

Powell told him, and the answer was the same as it had been from the beginning: no progress.

At 4:30 Malcolm decided it was time to steal a car. He had considered many other ways of obtaining transportation, but crossed them off his list as too risky. Providence com-

bined with the American Legion and a Kentucky distillery
to solve Malcolm's problem.

If it hadn't been for the American Legion and their
National Conference on Youth and Drugs, Alvin Phillips
would never have been in Washington, let alone at the
Washington Monument. He was chosen by the Indiana state
commander to attend the expense-paid national conference
to learn all he could about the evils of drug abuse among the
young. While at the conference, he had been given a pass
which would enable him to avoid the lines at the Monument
and go straight to the top. He lost this pass the night before,
but he felt obligated to at least see the Monument for the
folks back home.

If it hadn't been for a certain Kentucky distillery, Alvin
would not have been in his present state of intoxication. The
distillery kindly provided all conference participants with a
complimentary fifth of their best whiskey. Alvin had become so upset by the previous day's film describing how
drugs often led to illicit sex among nubile teen-age girls that
the night before he drank the entire bottle by himself in his
Holiday Inn room. He liked the whiskey so much that he
bought another fifth to help him through the conference and
"kill the dog that bit him." He finished most of that fifth by
the time the meetings broke up and he managed to navigate
to the Monument.

Malcolm didn't find Alvin, Alvin found the line. Once
there, he made it plain to all who could hear that he was
standing in this hot God damn sun out of patriotic duty. He
didn't have to be here, he could have gone right to the God
damn top, except for that God damn hustling floozy who
lifted his wallet and the God damn pass. He sure fooled her
God damn ass with those traveler's checks—best God damn

things you could buy. She sure had God damn big jugs, though. God damn it, all he wanted to do was take her for a ride in his new car.

When Malcolm heard the word "car," he immediately developed a dislike for cheap God damn floozies and a strong affection for the American Legion, Indiana, Kentucky whiskey, and Alvin's brand-new Chrysler. After a few short introductory comments, he let Alvin know he was talking to a fellow veteran of American wars, one whose hobby just happened to be automobiles. Have another drink, Alvin, old buddy.

"S'at right? You really dig cars?" The mention of important matters pulled Alvin part way out of the bottle. It didn't take a lot of effort for bosom companionship to slide him back down. "You wanna see a real good 'un? Got me bran'-new one. Jus' drove 't here from Indiana. Ever been to Indiana? Gotta come, come see me. An' the old lady. She ain't much to look at—we're forry-four, you know. I don't look forry-four, do I? Where was I? Oh yeah, ol' lady. Good woman. A li'l fat, but what the hell, I always say . . ."

By this time Malcolm had maneuvered Alvin away from the crowd and into a parking lot. He had also shared half a dozen swigs from the bottle Alvin carefully kept hidden under his soggy suit coat. Malcolm would raise the bottle to his closed lips and move his Adam's apple in appreciation. He didn't want alcohol slowing him down for the night. When Alvin took his turn, he more than made up for Malcolm's abstention. By the time they reached the parking lot, only two inches remained in the bottle.

Malcolm and Alvin talked about those God damn kids and their God damn drugs. Especially the girls, the teen-age girls, just like the cheerleaders in Indiana, hooked on that marijuana and ready to do anything, "anything," for that God damn drug. Anything. Malcolm casually mentioned that he knew where two such girls were hanging around, just waiting to do anything for that God damn marijuana. Alvin stopped him and plaintively said, "Really?" Alvin thought very hard when Malcolm ("John") assured him that such was the case. Malcolm let the discussion lag, then he helped Alvin suggest meeting these two girls so Alvin could tell the folks back in Indiana what it was really like. Really like. Since the girls were in kind of a public place, it probably would be best if "John" went and picked them up and brought them back here. Then they could all go to Alvin's room and talk. Better to talk to them there than here. Find out why they'd do anything, *anything*, for that God damn marijuana. Alvin gave Malcolm the keys just as they reached the shiny new car.

"Got lotsa gas, lotsa gas. Sure ya don't need any money?" Alvin fumbled with his clothes and extracted a weather-beaten wallet. "Take watcha need, bitch last night only got traveler's checks." Malcolm took the wallet. While Alvin shakily tipped the bottle to his lips, his new friend removed all identification papers from the wallet, including a card with his car license number. He gave the wallet back to Alvin.

"Here," he said. "I don't think they'll want any money. Not now." He smiled briefly, secretively. When Alvin saw the smile his heart beat a shade faster. He was too far gone to show much facial expression.

Malcolm unlocked the car. A crumpled blue cap lay on the front seat. On the floor was a six-pack of beer Alvin had brought to help ease the heat. Malcolm put the cap on his friend's head and exchanged the now empty whiskey bottle for the six-pack of beer. He looked at the flushed face and blurred eyes. Two hours in the sun and Alvin should pass out. Malcolm smiled and pointed to a grassy mall.

"When I come back with the girls, we'll meet you over there, then go to your room. You'll recognize us because they both have big jugs. I'll be back with them just after you finish the six-pack. Don't worry about a thing." With a kindly push he sent Alvin staggering off to the park and the tender mercies of the city. When he pulled out of the parking lot, he glanced at the rearview mirror in time to see Alvin lurch to a sitting position on a portion of grass well away from anyone else. Malcolm turned the corner as Alvin opened a beer can and took a long, slow swig.

The car had almost a full tank of gas. Malcolm drove to the expressway circling the city. He stopped briefly at a drive-in restaurant in Chevy Chase for a cheeseburger and use of the rest room. In addition to relieving himself, he checked his gun.

Number 42 Elwood Lane was indeed a country estate. The house was barely visible from the road. Direct access to it was through a private lane closed off by a stout iron gate. The closest neighboring house was at least a mile away. Dense woods surrounded the house on three sides. The land between the house and the road was partially cleared. From Malcolm's brief glance he could tell that the house was large, but he didn't stop for a closer look. That would be foolish.

From a small gas station just up the road he obtained a map of the area. The woods behind the house were uninhabited hills. When he told the gas-station attendant he was a vacationing ornithologist and that he might have seen a very rare thrush, the attendant helped him by describing some unmapped country roads which might lead to the bird's nesting area. One such road ran behind 42 Elwood Lane.

Because of the attendant's anxious help, Malcolm found the proper road. Bumpy, unpaved, and with only traces of gravel, the road wound around hills, through gullies, and over ancient cowpaths. The woods were so dense that at times Malcolm could see only twenty feet from the road. His luck held, though, and when he topped a hill he saw the house above the trees to his left, at least a mile away. Malcolm pulled the car off the road, bouncing and lurching into a small clearing.

The woods were quiet, the sky was just turning pink. Malcolm quickly pushed his way through the trees. He knew he had to get close to the house before all light faded or he would never find it.

It took him half an hour of hard work. As the day shifted from sunset to twilight, he reached the top of a small hill. The house was just below him, three hundred yards away. Malcolm dropped to the ground, trying to catch his breath in the crisp, fresh air. He wanted to memorize all he could see in the fading light. Through the windows of the house he caught fleeting glimpses of moving figures. The yard was big, surrounded by a rock wall. There was a small shed behind the house.

He would wait until dark.

Inside the house Robert Atwood sat back in his favorite easy chair. While his body relaxed, his mind worked. He did not want to meet with Maronick and his men tonight, especially not here. He knew the pressure was on them, and he knew they would press him for some sort of alternate solution. At present Atwood didn't have one. The latest series of events had changed the picture considerably. So much depended on the girl. If she regained consciousness and was able to identify him . . . well, that would be unfortunate. It was too risky to send Maronick after her, the security precautions were too tight. Atwood smiled. On the other hand, the girl's survival might pose some interesting and favorable developments, especially in dealing with Maronick. Atwood's smile broadened. The infallible Maronick had missed. True, not by much, but he had missed. Perhaps the girl, a living witness, might be useful against Maronick. Just *how* Atwood wasn't sure, but he decided it might be best if Maronick continued thinking the girl was dead. She could be played later in the game. For the time being Maronick must concentrate on finding Malcolm.

Atwood knew Maronick had insisted on meeting him at his home in order to commit him even further. Maronick would make it a point to be seen by someone in the neighborhood whom the police might later question should things go wrong. In this way Maronick sought to further ensure Atwood's loyalty. Atwood smiled. There were ways around that one. Perhaps the girl might prove a useful lever there. If . . .

"I'm going now, dear." Atwood turned toward the speaker, a stocky gray-haired woman in an expensively cut suit. He rose and walked with his wife to the door. When he was close to his wife, his eyes invariably traveled to the tiny scars on her neck and the edge of her hairline where the plastic surgeon had stretched and lifted years from her skin. He smiled, wondering if the surgery and all her hours at an exclusive figure salon made her lover's task any more agreeable.

Elaine Atwood was fifty, five years younger than her

husband and twenty-four years older than her lover. She knew the man who had driven her wild and brought back her youth as Adrian Queens, a British graduate student at American University. Her husband knew all about her lover, but he knew that Adrian Queens was really Alexy Ivan Podgovich, an aspiring KGB agent who hoped to milk the wife of a prominent American intelligence officer for information necessary to advance his career. The "affair" between Podgovich and his wife amused him and served his purposes very well. It kept Elaine busy and distracted and provided him with an opportunity to make an intelligence coup of his own. Such things never hurt a man's career, if he knows how to take advantage of opportunity.

"I may just stay over at Jane's after the concert, darling. Do you want me to call?"

"No, dear, I'll just assume you are with her if you aren't home by midnight. Don't worry about me. Give Jane my love."

The couple emerged from the house. Atwood delivered a perfunctory kiss to his wife's powdered cheek. Before she reached the car in the driveway (a sporty American car, not the Mercedes) her mind was on her lover and the long night ahead. Before Atwood closed the front door his mind was back on Maronick.

Malcolm saw the scene in the doorway, although he couldn't discern features at that distance. The wife's departure made his confidence surge. He would wait thirty minutes.

Fifteen of that thirty minutes had elapsed when Malcolm realized there were two men walking up the driveway toward the house. Their figures barely stood out from the shadows. If it hadn't been for their motion, Malcolm would never have seen them. The only thing he could distinguish from his distant perch was the tall leanness of one of the men. Something about the tall man triggered Malcolm's subconscious, but he couldn't pull it to the surface. The men, after ringing the bell, vanished inside the house.

With binoculars, Malcolm might have seen the men's car. They had parked it just off the road inside the gate and walked the rest of the way. Although he wanted to leave traces of his visit to Atwood's house, Maronick saw no point in letting Atwood get a look at their car.

Malcolm counted to fifty, then began to pick his way toward the house. Three hundred yards. In the darkness it was hard to see tree limbs and creepers reaching to trip him and bring him noisily down. He moved slowly, ignoring the scratches from thornbushes. Halfway to the house, Malcolm stumbled over a stump, tearing his pants and wrenching his knee, but somehow he kept from crying out. One hundred yards. A quick, limping dash through brush stubble and long grass before he crouched behind the stone wall. Malcolm eased the heavy magnum into his hand while he fought to regain his breath. His knee throbbed, but he tried not to think about it. Over the stone wall lay the house yard. In the yard to the right was the crumbling tool shed. A few scattered evergreens stood between him and the house. To his left was blackness.

Malcolm looked at the sky. The moon hadn't risen yet. There were few clouds and the stars shone brightly. He waited, catching his breath and assuring himself his ears heard nothing unusual in the darkness. He vaulted the low wall and ran to the nearest evergreen. Fifty yards.

A shadow quietly detached itself from the tool shed to

swiftly merge with an evergreen. Malcolm should have noticed. He didn't.

Another short dash brought Malcolm to within twenty-five yards of the house. Glow from inside the building lit up all but a thin strip of grass separating him and the next evergreen. The windows were low. Malcolm didn't want to chance a fleeting glance to the outside catching him running across the lawn. He sprawled to his belly and squirmed across the thin shadowed strip. Ten yards. Through open windows he could hear voices. He convinced himself different noises were his imagination playing on Mother Nature.

Malcolm took a deep breath and made a dash for the bush beneath the open window. As he was taking his second step, he heard a huffing, rushing noise. The back of his neck exploded into reverberating fire.

"The truth, the whole truth, and nothing but the truth."

—*Traditional oath*

Late Tuesday Night, Early Wednesday Morning

Consciousness returned abruptly to Malcolm. He felt a dim awareness around his eyes, then suddenly his body telegraphed a desperate message to his brain: he had to vomit. He lurched forward, up, and had his head thrust into a thoughtfully provided bucket. When he stopped retching, he opened his aching eyes to take in his plight.

Malcolm blinked to clear his contacts. He was sitting on the floor of a very plush living room. In the opposite wall was a small fireplace. Two men sat in easy chairs between him and that wall. The man who shot Wendy and his companion. Malcolm blinked again. He saw the outline of a man on his right. The man was very tall and thin. As he turned to take a closer look, the man behind him jerked Malcolm's head so he again faced the two seated men. Malcolm tried to move his hands, but they were tied behind his back with a silk tie that would leave no marks.

The older of the two men smiled, obviously very pleased with himself. "Well, Condor," he said, "welcome to my nest."

The other man was almost impassive, but Malcolm thought he saw curious amusement in the cold eyes.

The older man continued. "It has taken us a long time to find you, dear Malcolm, but now that you are here, I'm really rather glad our friend Maronick didn't shoot you too. I have some questions to ask you. Some questions I already know the answers to, some I don't. This is the perfect time to get those answers. Don't you agree?"

Malcolm's mouth was dry. The thin man held a glass of water to his lips. When Malcolm finished, he looked at the two men and rasped, "I have some questions too. I'll trade you answers."

The older man smiled as he spoke. "My dear boy. You don't understand. I'm not interested in your questions. We won't even waste our time with them. Why should I tell you anything? It would be so futile. No, you shall talk to us. Is he ready yet, Cutler, or did you swing that rifle a little too hard?''

The man holding Malcolm had a deep voice. ''His head should be clear by now.'' With a quick flick of his powerful wrists the man pulled Malcolm down to the floor. The thin man pinned Malcolm's feet, and Maronick pulled down Malcolm's pants. He inserted a hypodermic needle into Malcolm's tensed thigh, sending the clear liquid into the main artery. It would work quicker that way, and the odds that a coroner would notice a small injection on the inside of a thigh are slim.

Malcolm knew what was happening. He tried to resist the inevitable. He forced his mind to picture a brick wall, to feel a brick wall, smell a brick wall, become a brick wall. He lost all sense of time, but the bricks stood out. He heard the voices questioning him, but he turned their sounds to bricks for his wall.

Then slowly, piece by piece, the truth serum chiseled away at the wall. His interrogators carefully swung their hammers. Who are you? How old are you? What is your mother's name? Small, fundamental pieces of mortar chipped away. Then bigger hunks. Where do you work? What do you do? One by one, bricks pried loose. What happened last Thursday? How much do you know? What have you done about it? Why have you done it?

Little by little, piece by piece, Malcolm felt his wall crumble. While he felt regret, he couldn't will the wreckage to stop. Finally his tired brain began to wander. The questions stopped and he drifted into a void. He felt a slight prick on his thigh and the void filled with numbness.

Maronick made a slight miscalculation. The mistake was understandable, as he was dealing with milligrams of drugs to obtain results from an unknown variable, but he should have erred on the side of caution. When he secretly squirted out half the dosage in the syringe Atwood gave him, Maronick thought he had still used enough to produce unconsciousness. He was a little short. The drug combined with the sodium pentothal as predicted, but it was only strong enough to cause stupor, not unconsciousness.

Malcolm was in a dream. His eyelids hung low over his contacts, but they wouldn't shut. Sounds came to him through a stereo echo box. His mind couldn't connect, but it could record.

—Shall we kill him now? (The deep voice.)

—No, on the scene.

—Who?

—I'll let Charles do it, he likes blood. Give him your knife.

—Here, you give it to him. I'll check this again.

Receding footsteps. A door opens, closes. Hands running over his body. Something brushes his face.

—Damn.

A pink slip of paper on the floor by his shoulder. The tears fogging his contacts, but on the paper, "#27, TWA, National, 6 A.M."

The door opens, closes. Footsteps approaching.

—Where are Atwood and Charles?

—Checking the grounds in case he dropped anything.

—Oh. By the way, here's that reservation I made for you. James Cooper.

Paper rustles.

—Fine, let's go.

Malcolm felt his body lift off the floor. Through rooms. Outside to the cooling night air. Sweet smells, lilacs blooming. A car, into the back seat. His mind began to record more details, close gaps. His body was still lost, lying on the floor with a pair of heavy shoes pressed in his back. A long, bumpy ride. Stop. Engine dies and car doors open.

—Charles, can you carry him into the woods, up that way, maybe fifty yards. I'll bring the shovel in a few minutes. Wait until I get there. I want it done a certain way.

A low laugh. —No trouble.

Up into the air, jammed onto a tall, bony shoulder, bouncing over a rough trail, pain jarring life back into the body.

By the time the tall man dropped Malcolm on the ground, consciousness had returned. His body was still numb, but his mind was working and his eyes were bright. He could see the tall man smile in the dimly lit night. His eyes found the source of the series of clicks and snaps cutting through the humid air. The man was opening and closing the switchblade in eager anticipation.

Twigs snapped and dead leaves crunched under a light foot. The striking man appeared at the edge of the small clearing. His left hand held a flashlight. The beam fell on Malcolm as he tried to rise. The man's right hand hung close to his side. His clear voice froze Malcolm's actions. "Is our Condor all right?"

The tall man broke in impatiently. "He's fine, Maronick, as if it mattered. He sure came out of that drug quickly." The thin man paused to lick his lips. "Are you ready now?"

The flashlight beam moved to the tall man's eager face. Maronick's voice came softly through the night air. "Yes, I am." He raised his right arm and with a soft *plop!* from the silencer shot the tall man through the solar plexus.

The bullet buried itself in Charles's spine. The concussion

knocked him back on his heels, but he slumped forward to his knees, then to his face. Maronick walked over to the long, limp form. To be very sure, he fired one bullet through the head.

Malcolm's mind reeled. He knew what he saw, but he didn't believe it. The man called Maronick walked slowly toward him. He bent over and checked the bonds that held Malcolm's feet and hands. Satisfied, he sat on a handily placed log, turned off the flashlight, and said, "Shall we talk?

"You stumbled into something and you blundered your way through it. I must say I've developed a sort of professional admiration for you during the last five days. However, that has nothing to do with my decision to give you a chance to come out of this alive—indeed, a hero.

"In 1968, as part of their aid to a beleaguered, anti-communist government, the CIA assisted certain Meo tribes in Laos with the main commercial activity of that area, narcotics production. Mixed among all the fighting going on in that area there was a war between competing commercial factions. Our people assisted one faction by using transport planes to move the unprocessed opiate product along its commercial route. The whole thing was very orthodox from a CIA point of view, though I imagine there are many who frown on the U.S. government pushing dope.

"As you know, such enterprises are immensely profitable. A group of us, most of whom you have met, decided that the opportunity for individual economic advancement was not to be overlooked. We diverted a sizable quantity of high-quality heroin from the official market and channeled it into another source. We were well rewarded for our labor.

"I disagreed with Atwood's handling of the matter from

the start. Instead of unloading the stuff in Thailand and taking a reasonable profit, he insisted on exporting the heroin directly to the States and selling it to a U.S. group who wanted to avoid as many middlemen as possible. To do that, we needed to use the Agency more than was wise.

"We used your section for two purposes. We compromised a bursar—not your old accountant—to juggle and later rejuggle the books and get us seed money. We then shipped the heroin Stateside in classified book cases. The bags fit quite nicely into those boxes, and since they were shipped as classified materials, we didn't have to worry about customs inspection. Our agent in Seattle intercepted the shipment and delivered it to the buyers. But this background has little to do with your being here.

"Your friend Heidegger started it all. He had to get curious. In order to eliminate the possibility that someone might find something fishy, we had to eliminate Heidegger. To cover his death and just in case he told someone else, we had to hit the whole section. But you botched our operation through blind luck."

Malcolm cleared his throat. "Why are you letting me live?"

Maronick smiled. "Because I know Atwood. He won't feel safe until my associates and I are dead. We're the only ones who can link him to the whole mess. Except you. Consequently, we have to die. He is probably thinking of a way to get rid of us. We are supposed to pick up those envelopes at the bank tomorrow. I'm quite sure we would be shot in a holdup attempt, killed in a car wreck, or just 'disappear.' Atwood plays dumb, but he's not."

Malcolm looked at the dark shape on the ground. "I still don't understand. Why did you kill that man Charles?"

"I like to cover my tracks too. He was dangerous dead weight. It will make no difference to me who reads the letters. The powers-that-be already know I'm involved. I shall quietly disappear to the Middle East, where a man of my talents can always find suitable employment.

"But I don't want to turn a corner someday and find American agents waiting for me, so I'm giving the country a little present in hopes it will regard me as a sheep gone astray but not worth chasing. My farewell present—Robert Atwood. I'm letting you live for somewhat the same reason. You also have the chance to deliver Mr. Atwood. He has caused you a lot of grief. After all, it was he who necessitated all those deaths. I am merely a technician like yourself. Sorry about the girl, but I had no option. *C'est la guerre*."

Malcolm sat for a long time. Finally he said, "What's the immediate plan?"

Maronick stood. He threw the switchblade at Malcolm's feet. Then he gave him still another injection. His voice was impassive. "This is an extremely strong stimulant. It would put a dead man on his feet for half a day. It should give you enough oomph to handle Atwood. He's old, but he's still very dangerous. When you cut yourself free, get back to the clearing where we parked the car. In case you didn't notice, it's the same one you used. There are one or two things that might help you in the back seat. I would park just outside his gate, then work my way to the rear of the house. Climb the tree and go in through the window on the second floor. It somehow got unlocked. Do what you like with him. If he kills you, there are still the letters and several corpses for him to explain."

Maronick looked down at the figure by his feet. "Goodbye, Condor. One last word of advice. Stick to research. You've used up all your luck. When it comes right down to it, you're not very good." He vanished in the woods.

After a few minutes of silence, Malcolm heard a car start and drive away. He wormed his way toward the knife.

It took him half an hour. Twice he cut his wrists, but each time it was only minor and the bleeding stopped as soon as he quit using his hands.

He found the car. There was a note taped to the window. The body of the man called Cutler sprawled by the door. He had been shot in the back. The note had been written while the tall man carried Malcolm into the woods. It was short, to the point: "Your gun jammed with mud. Rifle in back has 10 rds. Hope you can use automatic."

The rifle in back was an ordinary .22 varmint rifle. Cutler had used it for target practice. Maronick left it for Malcolm, as he figured any amateur could handle so light a weapon. He left the automatic pistol with silencer just in case. Malcolm ripped the note off and drove away.

By the time he coasted the car to a stop outside Atwood's gate, Malcolm felt the drug taking effect. The pounding in the back of his neck and head, the little pains in his body, all had vanished. In their place was a surging, confident energy. He knew he would have to fight the overestimation and overconfidence the drug brought.

The oak tree proved simple to climb and the window was unlocked. Malcolm unslung the rifle. He worked the bolt to arm the weapon. Slowly, quietly, he tiptoed to the dark hall, down the carpeted hallway to the head of the stairs. He heard Tchaikovsky's "1812" Overture booming from the room where he had been questioned. Every now and then a triumphant hum would come from a familiar voice. Slowly Malcolm went down the stairs.

Atwood had his back to the door when Malcolm entered the room. He was choosing another record from the rack in the wall. His hand paused on Beethoven's Fifth.

Malcolm very calmly raised the rifle, clicked off the safety, took aim, and fired. Hours of practice on gophers, rabbits, and tin cans guided the bullet home. It shattered Atwood's right knee, bringing him screaming to the floor.

Terror and pain filled the old man's eyes. He rolled over in time to see Malcolm work the action again. He screamed as Malcolm's second bullet shattered his other knee. His mouthed framed the question, "Why?"

"Your question is futile. Let's just say I didn't want you going anywhere for a while."

Malcolm moved in a frenzy of activity. He tied towels around the moaning man's knees to slow the bleeding; then he tied his hands to an end table. He ran upstairs and aimlessly rifled rooms, burning up the energy coursing through his blood. He fought hard and was able to control his mind. Maronick chose his drugs well, he thought. Atwood the planner, the director, the thinker was downstairs, Malcolm thought, in pain and harmless. The secondary members of the cell were all dead. Maronick was the only one left, Maronick the enforcer, Maronick the killer. Malcolm thought briefly of the voices on the other end of the Panic Line, the professionals, professionals like Maronick. No, he thought, so far it has been me. Them against me. Maronick had made it even more personal when he killed Wendy. To the professionals it was just a job. They didn't care. Hazy details of a plan formed around his ideas and wants. He ran to Atwood's bedroom, where he exchanged his tattered clothes for one of several suits. Then he visited the kitchen and devoured some cold chicken and pie. He went back to the room where Atwood lay, took a quick look around, then dashed to his car for the long drive.

Atwood lay very still for some time after Malcolm had left. Slowly, weakly, he tried to pull himself and the table across the floor. He was too weak. All he succeeded in doing was knocking a picture off the table. It fell face up. The glass didn't break into shreds he could use to cut his bonds. He resigned himself to his fate. He slumped prone, resting for whatever might lie ahead. He looked briefly at the picture and sighed. It was of him. In his uniform of a captain in the United States Navy.

"Employees must wash their hands before leaving."

—*Traditional rest-room sign*

Wednesday Morning

Mitchell had reached what Agency psychiatrists call the Crisis Acclimatization Level, or Zombie Stage 4. For six days he had been stretched as tight as any spring could be stretched. He adjusted to this state and now accepted the hypertension and hyperactivity as normal. In this state he would be extremely competent and extremely effective as long as any challenge fell within the context of the conditions causing the state. Any foreign stimulus would shatter his tensed composure and tear him apart at the seams. One of the symptoms of this state is the ignorance of the subject. Mitchell merely felt a little nervous. His rational process told him he must have overcome the exhaustion and tension with a sort of second wind. That was why he was still awake at 4:20 in the morning. Disheveled and smelly from six days without bathing, he sat behind his desk going over reports for the hundredth time. He hummed softly. He had no idea that the two additional security men standing by the coffee urn were for him. One was his backup and the other was a psychiatrist protégé of Dr. Lofts. The psychiatrist was there to watch Mitchell as well as monitor any of Malcolm's calls.

Brrring!

The call jerked all the men in the room out of relaxation. Mitchell calmly held up one hand to reassure them while he used the other hand to pick up the receiver. His easy movements had the quiet quickness of a natural athlete or a well-oiled machine.

"493–7282."

"This is Condor. It's almost over."

"I see. Then why don't you . . ."

"I said almost. Now listen, and get it right. Maronick, Weatherby, and their gang were working under a man called Atwood. They were trying to cover their tracks from a smuggling operation they pulled off in 1968. They used Agency facilities and Heidegger found out. The rest just sort of came naturally.

"I've got one chore left. If I don't succeed, you'll know

about it. At any rate, I've mailed some stuff to my bank. You better pick it up. It will be there this morning.

"You better send a pretty good team to Atwood's right away. He lives at 42 Elwood Lane, Chevy Chase." (Mitchell's second picked up a red phone and began to speak softly. In another part of the building men raced toward waiting cars. A second group raced toward a Cobra combat helicopter kept perpetually ready on the building roof.) "Send a doctor with them. Two of Maronick's men are in the woods behind the house, but they're dead. Wish me luck."

The phone clicked before Mitchell could speak. He looked at his trace man and got a negative shake of the head.

The room burst into activity. Phones were lifted and all through Washington people woke to the shrill ring of a special bell. Typewriters clicked, messengers ran from the room. Those who could find nothing definite to do paced. The excitement around him did not touch Mitchell. He sat at his desk, calmly running through the developed procedure. His forehead and palms were dry, but deep in his eyes a curious light burned.

Malcolm depressed the phone hook and inserted another dime. The buzzer only sounded twice.

The girl had been selected for her soft, cheery voice. "Good morning. TWA. May I help you?"

"Yes, my name is Henry Cooper. My brother is flying out today for an overdue vacation. Getting away from it all, you understand. He didn't tell anyone where he was going for sure because he hadn't made up his mind. What we want to do is give him a last-minute going-away present. He's already left his apartment, but we think he's on Flight 27, leaving at six. Could you tell me if he has a reservation?"

There was a slight pause, then, "Yes, Mr. Cooper, your brother has booked a reservation on that flight for . . . Chicago. He hasn't picked up his ticket yet."

"Fine, I really appreciate this. Could you do me another favor and not tell him we called? The surprise is named Wendy, and there's a chance she'll be either flying with him or taking the next plane."

"Of course, Mr. Cooper. Shall I make a reservation for the lady?"

"No, thank you. I think we better wait and see how it works out at the airport. The plane leaves at six right?"

"Right."

"Fine, we'll be there. Thank you."

"Thank you, sir, for thinking of TWA."

Malcolm stepped out of the phone booth. He brushed some lint off his sleeve. Atwood's uniform fitted him fairly well, though it was somewhat bulky. The shoes were a loose fit and his feet tended to slip in them. The highly polished leather creaked as he walked from the parking lot into the main lobby of National Airport. He carried the raincoat draped over his arm and pulled the hat low over his forehead.

Malcolm dropped an unstamped envelope addressed to the CIA in a mailbox. The letter contained all he knew, including Maronick's alias and flight number. The Condor hoped he wouldn't have to rely on the U.S. postal system.

The terminal was beginning to fill with the bustling people who would pass through it during the day. A wheezing janitor swept cigarette butts off the red rug. A mother tried to coax a bored infant into submission. A nervous coed sat wondering if her roommate's half-fare card would work. Three young Marines headed home to Michigan wondered if she would work. A retired wealthy executive and a penniless wino slept in adjoining chairs, both waiting for daughters to fly in from Detroit. A Fuller Brush executive sat perfectly still, bracing himself for the effects of a jet flight on a gin hangover. The programmer for the piped-in music had decided to jazz up the early-morning hours, and a nameless orchestra played watered-down Beatle music.

Malcolm strode to a set of chairs within hearing range of the TWA desk. He sat next to the three Marines, who respectfully ignored his existence. He held a magazine so it obscured most of his face. His eyes never left the TWA desk. His right hand slipped inside the Navy jacket to bring the silenced automatic out. He slipped his gun-heavy hand under the raincoat and settled back to wait.

At precisely 5:30 Maronick walked confidently through the main doors. The striking gentleman had developed a slight limp, the kind observers invariably try to avoid looking at and the kind they always watch. The limp dominates their impression and their mind blurs the other details their eyes record. A uniform often accomplishes the same thing.

Maronick had grown a mustache with the help of a theatrical-supply house, and when he stopped at the TWA desk Malcolm did not recognize him. But Maronick's soft voice drew his attention, and he strained to hear the conversation.

"My name is James Cooper. I believe you have a reservation for me."

The desk clerk flipped her head slightly to place the wandering auburn lock where it belonged. "Yes, Mr. Cooper, Flight 27 to Chicago. You have about fifteen minutes until boarding time."

"Fine." Maronick paid for his ticket, checked his one

bag, and walked aimlessly away from the counter. Almost empty, he thought. Good. A few servicemen, everything normal; mother and baby, normal; old drunks, normal; college girl, normal. No large preponderance of men standing around busily doing nothing. No one scurrying to phones, including the girl behind the desk. Everything normal. He relaxed even more and began to stroll, checking the terminal and giving his legs the exercise they would miss on the long flight. He didn't notice the Navy captain who slowly joined him at a distance of twenty paces.

Malcolm almost changed his mind when he saw Maronick looking so confident and capable. But it was too late for that. Help might not arrive in time and Maronick might get away. Besides, this was something Malcolm had to do himself. He fought down the drug-edged nervousness. He would get only one chance.

National Airport, while not breathtakingly beautiful, is attractive. Maronick allowed himself to admire the symmetry of the corridors he passed through. Fine colors, smooth lines.

Suddenly he stopped. Malcolm barely had time to dodge behind a rack of comic books. The proprietress gave him a withering glance but said nothing. Maronick checked his watch and held a quick debate with himself. He would just have time. He began to move again, substituting a brisk walk for his leisurely stroll. Malcolm followed his example, carefully avoiding loud footsteps on the marble stretches. Maronick took a sudden right and passed through a door, which swung shut behind him.

Malcolm trotted to the door. His hand holding the gun under the raincoat was sweating from the heat, the drug, and his nerves. He stopped outside the brown door. Gentlemen.

He looked around him. No one. Now or never. Being careful to keep the gun between his body and the door, he pulled the weapon out from under the coat. He tossed the heavy raincoat to a nearby chair. Finally, his heart beating against his chest, he leaned on the door.

It opened easily and quietly. One inch. Malcolm could see the glistening white brightness of the room. Mirrors sparkled on the wall to his far left. He opened the door a foot. The wall with the door had a line of three shiny sinks. He could see four urinals on the opposite wall, and he could make out the corner of one stall. No one stood at the sinks or the urinals. Lemony disinfectant tingled his nose. He pushed the door open and stepped in. It closed behind him with a soft *whoosh* and he leaned heavily against it.

The room was brighter than the spring day outside the building. The piped-in music found no material capable of absorbing its volume, so the sound echoed off the tile walls—cold, crisp, blaring notes. There were three stalls opposite Malcolm. In the one on the far left he could see shoes, toes pointed toward him. Their polish added to the brightness of the room. The flute in the little box on the ceiling posed a gay musical question and the piano answered. Malcolm slowly raised the gun. The sound of toilet paper turning a spindle cued the band. The flute piped a more melancholy note as it inquired once more. A tiny click from the gun's safety preceded the sound of tearing paper and the piano's soft reply.

The gun jumped in Malcolm's hand. A hole tore through the thin metal stall door. Inside the stall the legs jerked, then pushed upward. Maronick, slightly wounded in the neck, desperately reached for the gun in his back pocket, but his pants were around his ankles. Maronick normally carried his gun holstered either at his belt or under his arm, but he had planned to ditch the weapon before passing through the security screening at the airport. There would probably be no need of a gun at this stage of the plan, especially at a large, crowded airport, but the cautious Maronick put his gun in his back pocket, unobtrusive but sometimes awkward to reach, just in case.

Malcolm fired again. Another bullet tore through screeching metal to bury itself in Maronick's chest and fling his body against the wall. Malcolm fired again, and again and again and again. The gun spat the spent cartridge cases onto the tile floor. Bitter cordite mixed with the lemony smell. Malcolm's third bullet ripped a hole through Maronick's stomach. Maronick sobbed softly, and fell down along the right side of the metal cage. His weakening arm depressed the plunger. The *woosh* of water and waste momentarily drowned out his sobs and the coughs from the gun. As Malcolm fired the fourth time, a passing stewardess hearing the muffled cough remembered it was cold season. She vowed to buy some vitamins. That bullet missed Maronick's sinking form. The lead shattered on the tile wall, sending little pieces of shrapnel into the metal walls and tile roof. A few hit Maronick's back, but they made no difference. Malcolm's fifth bullet buried itself on Maronick's left hip, positioning the dying man on the stool.

Malcolm could see the arms and feet of a man slumped on a toilet. A few red flecks stained the tile pattern. Slowly, almost deliberately, Maronick's body began to slide off the toilet. Malcolm had to be sure before he confronted the man's face, so he squeezed the trigger for the last two rounds. An awkward knee on a naked and surprisingly hairless leg jammed against a stall post. The body shifted slightly as it settled to the floor. Malcolm could see enough of the pale face. Death replaced Maronick's striking appearance with a rather common, glassy dullness. Malcolm dropped the gun to the floor. It skidded to a stop near the body.

It took Malcolm a few minutes to find a phone booth. Finally a pretty oriental stewardess helped the rather dazed naval officer. He even had to borrow a dime from her.

"493–7282." Mitchell's voice wavered slightly.

Malcolm took his time. In a very tired voice he said, "This is Malcolm. It's over. Maronick is dead. Why don't you send somebody to pick me up? I'm at National Airport. So is Maronick. I'm the guy in the Navy uniform by the Northwest terminal."

Three carloads of agents arrived two minutes ahead of the squad car summoned by the janitor who had found more than dirty toilets in his rest room.

"The whole is equal to the sum of its parts."

—*Traditional mathematical concept*

Wednesday Afternoon

"It was like shooting birds in a cage." The three men sipped their coffee. Powell looked at the smiling old man and Dr. Lofts. "Maronick didn't stand a chance."

The old man looked at the doctor. "Do you have any explanation for Malcolm's actions?"

The large man considered his answer, then said, "Without having talked to him at great length, no. Given his experiences of the last few days, especially the deaths of his friends and his belief that the girl was dead, his upbringing, training, and the general situation he found himself in, to say nothing of the drug's possible effect, I think his reaction was logical."

Powell nodded. He turned to his superior and said, "How's Atwood?"

"Oh, he will live, for a while at least. I always wondered about his oafishness. He did too well to be the idiot he played. He can be replaced. How are we handling Maronick's death?"

Powell grinned. "Very carefully. The police don't like it, but we've pressured them into accepting the idea that the Capitol Hill Killer committed suicide in the men's room of National Airport. Of course, we had to bribe the janitor to forget what he saw. No real problem, however."

A phone by the old man's elbow rang. He listened for a few moments, then hung up. He pushed the button next to the phone and the door opened.

Malcolm was coming down from the drug. He had spent three hours bordering on hysteria, and during that time he had talked continually. Powell, Dr. Lofts, and the old man heard six days compressed into three hours. They told him Wendy was alive after he finished, and when they took him to see her he was dazed by exhaustion. He stared at the peacefully sleeping form in the bright, antiseptic room and seemed not to be aware of the nurse standing beside him. "Everything will be fine." She said it twice but got no reaction. All Malcolm could see of Wendy was a small head swathed in bandages and a sheet-covered form connected by wires and plastic tubing to a complicated machine. "My God," he whispered with mixed relief and regret, "my God." They let him stand there in silence for several minutes before they sent him out to be cleaned up. Now he had on clothes from his apartment, but he looked strange even in them.

"Ah, Malcolm, dear boy, sit down. We won't keep you long." The old man was at his charming best, but he failed to affect Malcolm.

"Now, we don't want you to worry about a thing. Everything is taken care of. After you've had a nice long rest, we want you to come back and talk to us. You will do that, won't you, my boy?"

Malcolm slowly looked at the three men. To them his voice seemed very old, very tired. To him it seemed new. "I don't have much choice, do I?"

The old man smiled, patted him on the back, and, mumbling platitudes, led him to the door. When he returned to his seat, Powell looked at him and said, "Well, sir, that's the end of our Condor."

The old man's eyes twinkled. "Don't be so sure, Kevin, my boy, don't be so sure."